DAVE PORTER AT STAR RANCH

OR, THE COWBOY'S SECRET

I0617695

EDWARD STRATEMEYER

Dave Porter at Star Ranch

Edward Stratemeyer

© 1st World Library, 2007
PO Box 2211
Fairfield, IA 52556
www.1stworldlibrary.com
First Edition

LCCN: 2007923759

Softcover ISBN: 978-1-4218-4242-4
Hardcover ISBN: 978-1-4218-4144-1
eBook ISBN: 978-1-4218-4340-7

Purchase *"Dave Porter at Star Ranch"*
as a traditional bound book at:
www.1stWorldLibrary.com/purchase.asp?ISBN=978-1-4218-4242-4

1st World Library is a literary, educational organization
dedicated to:

- Creating a free internet library of downloadable ebooks

- Hosting writing competitions and offering book
publishing scholarships.

Interested in more 1st World Library books?
contact: literacy@1stworldlibrary.com
Check us out at: www.1stworldlibrary.com

1ˢᵗ World Library Literary Society

Giving Back to the World

"If you want to work on the core problem, it's early school literacy."

- James Barksdale, former CEO of Netscape

"No skill is more crucial to the future of a child, or to a democratic and prosperous society, than literacy."

- Los Angeles Times

Literacy... means far more than learning how to read and write... The aim is to transmit... knowledge and promote social participation."

- UNESCO

"Literacy is not a luxury, it is a right and a responsibility. If our world is to meet the challenges of the twenty-first century we must harness the energy and creativity of all our citizens."

- President Bill Clinton

"Parents should be encouraged to read to their children, and teachers should be equipped with all available techniques for teaching literacy, so the varying needs and capacities of individual kids can be taken into account."

- Hugh Mackay

PREFACE

"Dave Porter at Star Ranch" is a complete tale in itself, but forms the sixth volume in a line issued under the general title of "Dave Porter Series."

In the first book of the series, called "Dave Porter at Oak Hall," the reader was introduced to a typical American lad of to-day, and was likewise shown the workings of a modern boarding school—a little world in itself.

There was a cloud over Dave's parentage, and to solve the mystery he took a long sea voyage, as related in the second volume, called "Dave Porter in the South Seas." Then he came back to Oak Hall, to help win several important games, as the readers of "Dave Porter's Return to School" already know.

So far, although Dave had heard of his father, he had not met his parent. He resolved to go on a hunt for the one who was so dear to him, and what that led to was related in "Dave Porter in the Far North."

When Dave returned to America he was sent again to school—to dear old Oak Hall with its many associations. Here he met many friends and some enemies, as narrated in "Dave Porter and His Classmates." The lad had no easy time of it, but did something for the honor of the school that was a great credit to him.

While at Oak Hall, Dave, through his sister, received an

invitation to spend his coming summer vacation on a ranch in the Far West. He was privileged to take some friends with him; and how the invitation was accepted, and what happened, I leave the pages which follow to relate.

It has been an especial pleasure for me to write this book. During the past summer I covered about seven thousand miles of our great western country, and I have seen many of the places herein described. I have also been touched by our warm western hospitality, and have had the added pleasure of meeting some of my young readers face to face.

Once again I thank the many who have praised my books in the past. I trust that this volume may prove to their liking, and benefit them.

EDWARD STRATEMEYER.
April 12, 1910.

CONTENTS

CHAPTER I

DAVE AND HIS CHUMS

"Why, Dave, what are you going to do with that revolver?"

"Phil and Roger and I are going to do some target shooting back of the barn," answered Dave Porter. "If we are going to try ranch life, we want to know how to shoot."

"Oh! Well, do be careful!" pleaded Laura Porter, as she glanced affectionately at her brother. "A revolver is such a dangerous thing!"

"We know how to handle one. Phil has been painting a big door to represent a black bear, and we are going to see if we can do as well with a revolver as we did with the rifle."

"Do you expect to shoot bears on the ranch? I didn't see any when I was out there."

"We don't expect to see them around the house, but there must be plenty of game in the mountains."

"Oh, I presume that's true. But I shouldn't want to hunt bears—I'd be afraid," and Laura gave a little shiver.

"Girls weren't meant to be hunters," answered Dave, laughing. "But I shouldn't consider the outing complete unless I went on at least one big hunt—and I know Phil and Roger feel the same way about it."

"Hello, Dave!" cried a voice from an open doorway, and a handsome lad with dark curly hair showed himself. "Coming?"

"Yes, Roger. Where is Phil?"

"Gone to the field with his wooden bear." Roger Morr looked at his chum's sister. "Want to come along and try your luck?" he questioned. "A fine box of fudge to the one making the most bull's-eyes—I mean bear's-eyes."

"No, indeed, I'd be afraid of my life even to touch a revolver," answered the girl. "But I'll hunt up Jessie, and maybe we'll come down after a while to look on."

"Oh, you want to learn to shoot!" cried Roger. "Then, when we get to Star Ranch, you can dress up in regular cowgirl fashion, and ride a bronco, and fire off your gun in true western style."

"And have a big bear eat me up, eh?" answered Laura. "No, thank you—I want to come back East alive. But I'll come down to the field as soon as I can find Jessie," answered Laura, and walked away.

A long, melodious whistle was floating through the outside air, and Dave and Roger knew it came from Phil Lawrence. They hurried from the broad porch to the garden path, and around the corner of the carriage shed. Here they came upon their chum, carrying on his shoulder an old door upon which he had painted the upright figure of what was supposed to be a bear.

"Hurrah for the great animal painter!" cried Dave, as he ran up and took hold of one end of the door. "Phil, you ought to place this in the Academy of Design."

"It's superb!" was Roger's dry comment. "Best picture of a

kangaroo I ever saw. Or is it a sheep, Phil?"

"Humph! It's a good deal better than you could have painted," grumbled the amateur artist.

"Sure it is—best photo of a tiger I ever saw," said Dave, adding to the fun. "Why, you can almost hear him growl!"

"See here, if you're going to poke fun at me I'll throw the target away. I put in two hours of hard work, and three cans of paint, and—"

"We won't say another word, Phil," interrupted Roger. "Here, let me take hold. You've carried it far enough," and he relieved Phil of his burden.

"I wonder where would be the best place to set it?" mused Dave, gazing across the field.

"Up against the tree over there," answered Phil, pointing. "I had that spot picked out when I painted it. We'll set it so that it will look as if his bearship was trying to climb the tree."

"It's rather close to the back road," protested Dave. "We might hit somebody."

"Oh, hardly anybody uses that road,—so the stableman told me," answered Roger. "Besides, we can watch out. One always wants to be careful when shooting, at a target or otherwise."

The three youths soon had the target placed to their satisfaction, and then began a lively blazing away with the three revolvers that had been brought along. They aimed for the eyes of the painted creature, and for other vital spots, and all did fairly well.

"You're the best shot, Dave," announced Roger, during a lull in the practice, when all had gone to inspect the "damage" done. "You've plugged him right in the eyes three times and once in the heart. Had he been a real bear, he'd be as dead as a salt mackerel now."

"Provided he had consented to stand still," answered Dave. "Shooting at a stationary object is one thing, and at a moving, living creature quite another."

"I have it!" cried Phil. "Let us get a rope and throw it over one of the tree limbs. Then we can tie the door to it and swing it to and fro. We'll try to hit the bear while he's swinging."

"That's the talk!" returned Dave, enthusiastically. "I'll get the rope!" And he ran off to the barn for it. Little did he dream of what trouble that swinging target was to make for himself and his chums.

Many of my old readers already know Dave Porter, but for the benefit of others a brief outline of his past history will not be out of place. When he was a wee boy he had been found one day wandering along the railroad tracks outside of the village of Crumville. Nobody knew who he was or where he came from, and consequently he was put in the local poorhouse, there to remain until he was nine years old. Then a broken-down college professor named Caspar Potts, who was doing farming for his health, took the lad to live with him.

Caspar Potts gave Dave the rudiments of a good education. But he could not make his farm pay, and soon got into the grasp of Aaron Poole, a miserly money-lender, who threatened to sell him out.

Things looked exceedingly black for the old man and the boy when something very unexpected happened, as has been related in detail in the first volume of this series, called "Dave Porter at Oak Hall." In Crumville lived a rich manufacturer named Oliver Wadsworth, who had a beautiful daughter named Jessie, some years younger than Dave. Through an accident to the gasoline tank of an automobile, Jessie's clothing took fire, and she might have been burned to death had not

Dave rushed in and extinguished the flames.

Mr. Wadsworth was profuse in his thanks, and so was his wife, and both made inquiries concerning Dave and Caspar Potts. It was found that the latter was one of the manufacturer's former college professors, and Mr. Wadsworth insisted that Professor Potts give up farming and come and live with him, and bring Dave along. Then he sent Dave to boarding school, where the lad soon proved his worth, and made close chums of Roger Morr, the son of a United States senator; Phil Lawrence, the offspring of a wealthy shipowner, and a number of others.

The cloud concerning his parentage troubled Dave a great deal, and when he saw what he thought was a chance to clear up the mystery, he took a long trip from home, as related in "Dave Porter in the South Seas." After many adventures he found his uncle, Dunston Porter, and learned much concerning his father, David Breslow Porter, and his sister, Laura, then traveling in Europe.

Dave was now no longer a "poorhouse nobody," as some of his enemies had called him, but a well-to-do youth with considerable money coming to him when he should be of age. While waiting to hear from his parent he went back to Oak Hall, as related in "Dave Porter's Return to School." Here he added to his friends; yet some boys were jealous of his prosperity and did all they could to injure him. But their plots were exposed, and in sheer fright one of the lads ran away to Europe.

Much to Dave's disappointment, he did not hear from either his father or his sister. But he did receive word that the bully who had run away from Oak Hall had seen them, and so he resolved to go on another hunt for his relatives. As told in "Dave Porter in the Far North," he crossed the Atlantic with his chum, Roger, and followed his father to the upper part of Norway. Here at last the lonely lad met his parent face to face, a meeting as thrilling as it was interesting. He learned that his sister had returned to the United States, and with some friends named Endicott had gone to the latter's ranch in the Far West.

Mr. Oliver Wadsworth's mansion was a large one, and by an arrangement with him it was settled that, for the present, the Porters should make the place their home. All in a flutter of excitement, Laura came back from the West, and the meeting between brother and sister was as affecting as had been that between father and son. The girl brought with her some news that interested Dave deeply. It was to the effect that the ranch next to that of the Endicotts was owned by a Mr. Felix Merwell, the father of Link Merwell, one of Dave's bitterest enemies at Oak Hall. Link had met Laura out there and gotten her to correspond with him.

"It's too bad, Laura; I wish you hadn't done it," Dave had said on learning the news. "It may make trouble, for Merwell is no gentleman." And trouble it did make, as the readers of "Dave Porter and His Classmates" know. The trouble went from bad to worse, and not only were Laura and Dave involved, but also pretty Jessie Wadsworth and several of Dave's school chums. In the end Dave "took the law in his own hands" by giving Link Merwell a sound thrashing. Then some of the bully's wrongdoings reached the ears of the master of the school, and he was ordered to pack his trunk and leave, and a telegram was sent to his father in the West, stating that he had been expelled for violating the school rules. He left in a great rage.

"This is the work of that miserable poorhouse rat, Dave Porter," Link told some of his cohorts. "Just wait—I'll fix him for it some day, see if I don't!" Then he wrote a most abusive letter to Dave, but in his rage he forgot to address it properly, and it never reached the youth.

The term at Oak Hall came to an end in June and then arose the question of what to do during the vacation. In the meantime letters had been flying forth between Laura and her warm friend, Belle Endicott, who was still at Star Ranch, as Mr. Endicott's place was called. It may be said in passing that Mr. Endicott was a rich railroad president, and the ranch, while it

Edward Stratemeyer

paid well, was merely a hobby with him, and he and his family resided upon it only when it suited their fancy to do so.

"The Endicotts want me to come out again," said Laura to Dave. "They want me to bring you along with some of your chums, and they want me to bring Jessie, too, if her folks will let her come."

"Oh, that would be jolly!" Dave answered. When he thought of Jessie's going he blushed to himself, for to him the girl whose life he had once saved was the nicest miss in the whole world. Dave was by no means sentimental, but he had a warm, manly regard for Jessie that did him credit.

More letters passed back and forth, and it was finally arranged that Laura and Dave should visit Star Ranch during July and August, taking with them Jessie and Phil and Roger. Dunston Porter was to accompany the young folk as far west as Helena, near which the Endicotts were to meet the travelers, and then Dave's uncle was to go on to Spokane on business, coming back to take the young folks home about six weeks later.

The thoughts of spending their vacation on a real ranch filled the young folk with delight. All anticipated a "Jim-dandy" time, as Phil expressed it.

"We can go out hunting and fishing, and all that," declared the shipowner's son to his chums. "And maybe we'll bring down a bear or two." And then he suggested that they get revolvers and perfect themselves in marksmanship.

"Maybe we'll run into Link Merwell out there," said Roger. "My, but he was mad when he left Oak Hall! He'd like to chew your head off, Dave!"

"I don't want to see him," answered Dave, soberly. But this wish was not to be fulfilled. He was to meet Link Merwell in the near future, and that meeting was to be productive of some decidedly unpleasant results.

CHAPTER II

A STRAY SHOT

Dave soon returned to the field with a rope, and the representation of a bear was swung from the lower limb of an old apple tree. Then another smaller line was fastened at one side, so that the "bear" could be swung to and fro.

"You can do the first shooting," said Dave to his chums. "I'll play bellman." And he pulled on the side rope, so that the door swung like the pendulum of a clock.

"Hi! don't swing too fast!" called out Phil. "Sixty seconds to the minute, remember."

He took his position, and watching his chance, fired.

"How's that?" he asked, after the report had died away.

"Hit his bearship in the left ear," announced Dave.

"Humph! I aimed for his right eye!"

The senator's son now tried his luck and managed to hit the representation of a bear in the tail. This made all the lads laugh, and Roger and Phil called on Dave to show his skill.

"I don't think this revolver works very well," said the senator's son, handing the weapon to Dave. "The trigger seems to catch in some way."

"Oh, don't blame the pistol for your poor shooting, Roger!" cried Phil, good-naturedly.

"Well, examine the pistol for yourself, Phil."

Dave took the weapon and snapped the trigger. There was no report, and he tried again, aiming at some brushwood not far from the apple tree. The brushwood was close to the back road.

"It's all right now, I guess," he said, as the pistol went off with ease. "But that trigger ought to be looked after," he added. "You wouldn't want it to miss fire at a critical moment."

He stepped forward and, while Roger swung the representation of a bear, he fired another shot.

"Good for you!" exclaimed the senator's son in admiration. "You took him right in the throat, Dave!"

"Hold up there! Stop that! Do you hear me, you young rascals! Do you want to kill me?"

The call came from the back road, and looking in that direction, the three boys saw a well-dressed man coming toward them on the run. He was carrying a whip, and his face was full of sudden passion.

"It's Aaron Poole, Nat's father!" said Dave, as he lowered the pistol in his hand.

"I say, are you trying to kill me?" cried the miserly money-lender of Crumville, as he came closer, and he shook his whip at Dave.

"Why, no, Mr. Poole," answered Dave, as calmly as he could. "What makes you think that?"

"Oh, you needn't play innocent," snarled Aaron Poole. "You just fired a shot at me! It went through my buggy top." And the money-lender pointed to the back road, where stood his horse and carriage. "Nice doings, I must say!"

"Mr. Poole, I didn't fire at you," answered Dave. "I didn't know anybody was out there on the road,—and I didn't fire in that direction."

"You fired into the bushes, when you tried the pistol," said Roger, in a low voice.

"Maybe the bullet went through the bushes," suggested the shipowner's son.

"You fired at me—I heard the shot and saw you with the pistol!" stormed Aaron Poole. "I've a good mind to have you arrested!"

"Mr. Poole, why should I fire at you?" asked Dave. "I—"

"Oh, you needn't try to smooth it over, you young rascal! I know you! You are down on me because I made Caspar Potts pay me what was due, and you are down on my son Nat because he is more popular at Oak Hall than anybody else."

"Well, to hear that!" whispered Phil. He knew, as well as did the others, that overbearing Nat Poole had scarcely a friend left at the school the lads attended. On several occasions Nat had tried to harm Dave, but each time he had gotten the worst of it.

"I didn't fire at you—didn't know anybody was on the back road," protested Dave. "If a bullet went through your buggy top I am sorry for it, but I am also glad it didn't go through your head." And Dave had to shudder as he thought of what might have happened. "After this I'll be more careful when I shoot."

"Oh, don't you try to smooth it over!" snarled Aaron Poole. "I know you of old, Dave Porter! You are always up to some underhanded tricks. Nat knows you, too! Maybe you didn't mean to kill me, but you meant to scare me, and you took a big chance, for I might have been hit. I think I'll swear out a warrant for your arrest."

"Oh, Mr. Poole, don't do that!" cried Phil, in alarm. "Dave didn't know anybody was back there. It was purely an accident."

"Humph! Who are you, I'd like to know?"

"I am Phil Lawrence. I go to Oak Hall with Dave. I think we have met before."

"Oh, yes, I've heard of you—through my son, Nat. You sided with Porter against my son. Of course you'll stick up for Porter now. I think I'll go right down to town and get a warrant, and have it served." And the money-lender made as if to walk away.

"If you have Dave arrested we can testify that it was nothing but an accident," said Roger.

"Bah! it was no accident—he either meant to hit me or scare me! I'll have the law on him!" stormed Aaron Poole, and then he hurried away. Dave followed, wishing to argue the matter, but the money-lender would not listen, and leaping into his buggy he drove off at a rapid gait in the direction of Crumville Center.

"Now, I wonder what I had better do?" said Dave, soberly, after the angry man had departed.

"Do you really think he'll have you arrested?" questioned the senator's son.

"More than likely."

"But you didn't shoot at him. It was nothing but an accident."

"You can trust Mr. Poole to make out the blackest kind of a case against me," answered Dave, bitterly. "He has been down on me for years, and you know how Nat is down on me, too. He'll have me sent to prison, if he can!"

"We'll stand by you," said Phil. "We know you didn't shoot at him—or at anybody."

"I think I had better tell my father about this," went on Dave. All his interest in target-shooting had ended. "He will know what is best to do."

"We'll leave the target where it is," said Roger. "Then we can explain just how the thing occurred."

With downcast heart Dave left the field and approached the mansion, and his chums went with him. Just as they reached the piazza, the door opened and Laura came out, accompanied by Jessie Wadsworth.

"Oh, are you coming back?" asked Laura. "We were just going to join you."

"Maybe you've killed the bear!" cried Jessie, with a mischievous twinkle in her eyes. "I heard that Phil had manufactured one."

"No," answered Dave. "We—that is. I—had some trouble with Mr. Poole." He turned to his sister. "Where is father?"

"Gone out of town on business. He'll be back this evening."

"And Uncle Dunston?"

"Uncle went with him."

"Oh, that's too bad!" And Dave's face showed more concern

than ever.

"What was the trouble about?" asked Jessie, who was quick to see that Dave was ill at ease.

"Oh, Mr. Poole thought I shot at him—but I didn't," replied Dave, and then told the story.

"Oh, Dave, do you really think he'll have you locked up!" burst out his sister, while Jessie's face showed her deep concern.

"I don't know what he'll do," was the slow answer.

"Oh, maybe he won't do anything—after he calms down," said the shipowner's son. "He'll realize that Dave wouldn't do anything like that on purpose."

"You don't know Mr. Poole," said Jessie. "Father says he is one of the most hard-hearted men around here."

"Well, let us hope for the best," said the senator's son. He wanted to cheer up Laura and Jessie quite as much as Dave.

The boys put the pistols away and then went out in a summerhouse to talk the affair over.

"If he has me arrested, I suppose that will stop my going out to Star Ranch," said Dave, gloomily. "Too bad! And just when I was counting on having the time of my life!"

"Oh, don't take it so to heart, Dave!" cried Phil. "Maybe you'll never hear of it again."

"He'll hear of it if Mr. Poole tells Nat," said the senator's son. "Nat will want his father to make all the trouble possible for Dave."

"Where is Nat now? At home?"

"Yes," answered Dave. "I saw him yesterday, down at the post-office."

"Then he'll surely hear about it."

At first Dave thought to tell Caspar Potts about the affair, but then he realized that the professor was too old to aid him. Besides, the aged man was not well, and the boy hated to disturb him.

The middle of the afternoon came and went, and nothing was heard from Aaron Poole. Mrs. Wadsworth went out carriage-riding, taking the girls with her.

"Let us take a walk," proposed Phil. "No use in hanging around the house for nothing."

"I don't want Mr. Poole to think I ran away," answered Dave.

Nevertheless, he agreed to go with his chums, and they started off, leaving word that they would be back in time for dinner, which was served at the Wadsworth mansion at half-past six.

"I'd like to see that place where you used to live with Professor Potts," said the senator's son to Dave. "Is it far from here?"

"Quite a distance, but we can easily walk it," was the reply.

They passed out on the country road and were soon tramping along in the direction of the old Potts place. As they went on they talked over the proposed trip to the West.

"We ought surely to have the time of our lives," said the shipowner's son. "Just think of riding like the wind on some of those broncos!"

"Or getting flung heels over head from a bronco's back," added Roger. "I rather think we'll have to be careful at first."

"One thing I don't like about this trip," said Dave.

"The fact that Link Merwell's father owns the next ranch to the Star?"

"Exactly."

"Oh, ranch homes out there are sometimes miles apart," said Roger. "You may not see the Merwells at all."

"That will just suit me,—and I know it will suit Laura, too. She is awfully sorry that she once corresponded with Link."

"Well, she didn't know what he was," answered the senator's son. Ever since he had met Laura he had been much interested in Dave's sister.

The three chums had covered about half the distance to the old Potts place when they saw a horse and buggy approaching. As it came closer they saw that it contained two men.

"It's Mr. Poole!" cried Dave, and then, as he caught sight of the other man's face, he turned a trifle pale. "Step behind here!" he called to Phil and Roger, and pulled them back of some handy bushes.

The horse and buggy soon came up to them and passed on, the three boys keeping out of sight until the turnout was gone. Dave gave a deep sigh.

"I guess Mr. Poole means business," he said.

"What do you mean?" questioned the senator's son.

"I mean he is going to have me locked up."

"Why?" asked Phil.

"That man in the buggy with him was Mr. Mardell, the police justice."

Edward Stratemeyer

CHAPTER III

AN INTERVIEW OF INTEREST

"Well, I shouldn't go back home until your father and your uncle return," said the senator's son. "Then, if you are arrested, they'll know exactly what to do."

"It's too bad it happened!" murmured Dave. "I wish I had gotten off to the West without seeing Aaron Poole. But I suppose there is no use in crying over spilt milk. I'll have to face the music, and take what comes."

The three lads went on, and presently came in sight of the farm where Caspar Potts and Dave had once resided. The ground was now being cultivated by the man who had the next farm, and the house was tenantless.

"I've got the key of the house," said Dave. "If you'd like to take a look inside I'll unlock the door. But it's a very poor place—a big contrast to the Wadsworth residence."

"And so you used to work here, Dave?" said Phil, gazing around at the fields of corn and wheat.

"Yes, I've plowed and worked these fields more than once, Phil. And in those days, I didn't know what it was to have a nice suit of clothes and good food. But Professor Potts was kind to me, even if he was a bit eccentric."

"It was a grand thing that you found your folks—and your fortune," said Roger.

"Yes, and I am thankful from the bottom of my heart."

The three boys entered the deserted house, and Dave showed the way around. There was the same little cot on which he had been wont to stretch his weary limbs after a hard day's work in the fields, and there were the same simple cooking utensils with which he had prepared many a meal for himself and the old professor. Conditions certainly had improved wonderfully, and for the time being Dave forgot his trouble with Aaron Poole. No one could again call him "a poorhouse nobody."

From the cottage the boys walked to the barn. As they entered this building they heard earnest talking in the rear.

"You are a mean lad, to tease an old man like me!" they heard, in Caspar Potts's quavering tones. "Why cannot you go away and leave me alone?"

"Don't you call me mean!" came in Nat Poole's voice. "I'll do what I please, and you can't stop me!"

"I want you to leave me alone," reiterated the old professor.

"I will—when I am done with you. How do you like that, old man?" And then Nat Poole gave a brutal laugh.

"Oh! oh! Don't smother me!" spluttered Caspar Potts. "Please leave me alone! You have ruined my clothes!"

"I wonder what's up?" said Dave to his chums, and ran through the barn to the rear. There he beheld Caspar Potts in a corner. In front of him stood Nat Poole, holding a big garden syringe in his hands. The syringe had been filled with a preparation for spraying peach trees, and the son of the money-lender had discharged the chalk-like fluid all over the aged professor.

"Nat Poole, what are you up to!" cried Dave, indignantly, and, leaping forward, he caught the other youth by the shoulder and whirled him around. "You let Professor Potts alone!"

"Dave!" cried the professor, and his voice showed his joy. "Oh, I am glad you came. That young man has been teasing me for over a quarter of an hour, and he just covered me with that spray for the peach-tree scale."

"What do you mean by doing such a thing?" demanded Dave. "Give me that syringe." And he wrenched the article from the other youth's grasp. He looked so determined that Nat became alarmed and backed away several feet.

"Don't you—you—er—hit me!" cried the money-lender's son.

"What a mean piece of business," observed Roger, as he came up, followed by Phil. "Nat, you ought to be ashamed of yourself!"

"Oh, you shut up!" grumbled Nat, not knowing what else to say.

"I always thought you were a first-class coward," put in Phil. "Now I am sure of it."

"This is none of your affair, Phil Lawrence!"

"I should think it was the affair of any person who wanted to see fair play," answered the shipowner's son.

"Nat, you take your handkerchief and wipe off Mr. Potts's clothes," said Dave, sternly.

"Eh?" queried the money-lender's son in dismay.

"You heard what I said. Go and do it, and be quick about it."

"I—er—I don't have to."

"Yes, you do. If you don't—" Dave ended by walking over to a barrel and filling the syringe with the spraying fluid.

"Hi! don't you douse me with that!" yelled the other youth in alarm. Then he started to run away, but the senator's son caught him by one arm and Phil caught him by the other.

"You've got no right to hold me!"

"Well, we'll take the right," said Roger, calmly. "Now, Nat, do as Dave told you."

There was no help for it, and with very bad grace the money-lender's son drew from his pocket a silk handkerchief and removed what he could of the fluid from Caspar Potts's clothing. Many spots remained.

"I am afraid the suit is ruined," said the aged professor, sorrowfully. "Anyway, it will need a thorough cleaning."

"If it is ruined, Nat can pay for it," said Dave, firmly.

"I'll pay for nothing!" grumbled the boy who had done the mischief. He was short of spending-money, and knew how hard it was to get an extra dollar from his parent.

"He certainly ought to pay for it," said Caspar Potts. "Some men would have him locked up for what he has done."

"Humph! Don't talk foolish! It was only a little fun!" grumbled Nat. "I didn't mean any harm. You can easily get those spots out of your clothes."

"Did he do anything else to you?" asked Dave of the professor.

"Yes, he plagued me a good deal, and he shoved me down in the cow-yard," was the reply. "I was hoping some one would come to drive him away. I said I'd have the law on him, but he laughed at me, and said nobody else was around and his word

Edward Stratemeyer

was as good as mine."

"If that isn't Nat to a T!" murmured the senator's son. "Doing the sneak act every time!"

"Well, we are witnesses against him," put in Phil. He looked at Dave and suddenly began to grin. "Oh, but this is great!" he cried.

"What's struck you?" queried Dave.

"Oh, nothing, only I reckon we've got a good hold on Mr. Aaron Poole now—in case he tries to make a complaint against you."

"To be sure we have!" burst out Roger. "He won't dare to do it—after he knows what Professor Potts can do."

"What are you talking about?" demanded Nat, curiously. "Is my father going to make a complaint against Dave? What is it for?"

"Maybe you'll learn later—and maybe you won't," answered the senator's son. "But if you see your father you had better tell him to call it off as far as Dave is concerned—if he wants to save you."

"Then you've had trouble, eh?"

"No worse than this—if as bad."

"Humph! In that case my father won't believe what you say about me!" cried Nat, cunningly. And then of a sudden he leaped back, turned, and ran around a corner of the barn at top speed. He made for the road, and was soon hidden from view by trees and bushes. Phil and Roger attempted to catch him, but Dave called them back.

"No use in doing that," said Dave. "Let him go. It will be time enough to say more when Mr. Poole makes his complaint."

The three youths assisted Caspar Potts in rearranging his toilet, and in the meantime the aged professor told the lads the details of his trouble with Nat. The money-lender's son had certainly acted in a despicable manner, and he deserved to be punished.

"I will leave the matter to Mr. Wadsworth, and to your father and your uncle," said Professor Potts to Dave. "They will know better what to do than I."

On the way back to the Wadsworth mansion the boys told of the pistol incident and the professor became much interested. He agreed with Phil and Roger that Nat's doings were much worse.

Dave's father and his uncle had returned, and the youth went straight to them with his tale. Then Mr. Wadsworth came in and was likewise told. All the men were also informed of what had happened to Caspar Potts.

"I think I see a way of clearing this matter up—if Mr. Poole attempts to act against Dave," said Mr. Wadsworth. And then he had a long talk with Professor Potts.

The folks at the mansion had just finished dinner when visitors were announced. They proved to be Aaron Poole and an officer of the law, brought along to arrest Dave.

"I think you had better let me engineer this affair," said Mr. Wadsworth, and so it was agreed. He entered the reception room and shook hands formally with Aaron Poole.

"I came to get Dave Porter," said the money-lender, stiffly. "I am going to have him locked up."

"Mr. Poole, will you kindly step into the library with me?" answered Mr. Wadsworth.

"What for?"

"I wish to have a little conversation with you."

"It won't do any good. I'm going to have that Porter boy arrested, and that is all there is to it."

"I wished to see you about your son, Nat. Do you know that he stands in danger of arrest?"

"Arrest! Nat?" queried the money-lender, and the officer of the law looked at the rich manufacturer with interest.

"Yes. Come into the library, please."

"Want me?" asked the officer.

"No," returned Mr. Wadsworth, shortly, and the man settled back in his chair, his face showing his disappointment.

Once in the library the manufacturer shut the door with care. He motioned his visitor to a chair. But Aaron Poole was too impatient to sit down.

"Now, what's this about my son, Nat?" growled the money-lender.

"I'll tell you," was Mr. Wadsworth's reply, and he related what had occurred at the old Potts place.

"You expect me to believe this?" snarled Aaron Poole.

"Believe it or not, it is the truth, and I have the three boys to prove it, and likewise Professor Potts's ruined suit of clothing. Now," continued the manufacturer, "I know all about your charge against Dave. I'll not say that he wasn't careless, because he was. But he meant no harm, and it is going too far to have him arrested. It would be much fairer for Professor Potts to have your son locked up, and make you pay for the suit of clothing in the bargain. Now, the professor thinks a great deal of Dave, and he is willing to drop his complaint against Nat if you'll drop your complaint against Dave."

"Oh, so that's the way the wind blows, eh?" snarled Aaron Poole. "Well, I won't do it!" he snapped. "I'm going to have Dave Porter arrested!"

"If you do, Professor Potts will have Nat arrested, and we'll push our case just as hard as you push yours, Mr. Poole."

"Humph! I guess this is a plot to free Dave Porter!"

"You can think what you please. This is the way I look at it: Dave was careless, and his father can give him a lecture on his carelessness. Nat was brutal, and it is up to you to take him in hand. If he were my son, I'd give him a good talking to—and maybe I'd thrash him," added the rich manufacturer, warmly.

"Oh, you are all down on my son—just as you are down on me!" cried Aaron Poole. "I'll look into this! I'll—I'll—"

"Don't do anything hasty," advised Mr. Wadsworth. "Better talk the matter over with Nat."

"I'll do it. But I'll not drop this matter! I'll get after Dave Porter yet!" cried Aaron Poole, and then he stalked out of the library, and, motioning for the officer of the law to follow him, he left the mansion.

CHAPTER IV

CAUGHT IN THE ACT

"I don't think he'll do anything—that is, if he gets the truth out of Nat," said Mr. Wadsworth, as he rejoined the others. "Of course, if his son denies the attack on the professor, it may be different."

"If Nat does that, we'll have the testimony of the professor, Phil, and Roger against him," said Mr. Porter.

It must be admitted that the next day was an uncomfortable one for Dave, for he did not know at what moment an officer of the law might appear to arrest him. In the afternoon he and his chums went fishing, but he had little heart for the sport.

Early on the day following Ben Basswood called to see Dave and the others. As my old readers know, Ben had been a friend to Dave for many years, and had gone from Crumville to Oak Hall with him.

"Was coming before, to meet you and Roger and Phil," said Ben. "But I had to go out of town on business for dad. How are you all? Say, I hear you are going out West on a ranch. That's great! Going to shoot buffaloes, I suppose."

"No, hippopotamuses," put in the senator's son, with a grin.

"And June bugs," added Phil.

"You'll sure have the time of your lives! Wish I was going. But I am booked for the Great Lakes, which isn't bad. Going to take the trip from Buffalo to Duluth and back, you know. But say, I came over to tell you something."

"What is it, Ben?" questioned Dave.

"Come on outside."

The boys walked out into the garden and down to the summerhouse, where they proceeded to make themselves comfortable.

"It's about Nat Poole," continued Ben Basswood. "I guess you had some kind of a run-in with him, didn't you?"

"Not exactly," answered Roger. "We caught him tormenting Professor Potts and we put a stop to it."

"Well, you had some trouble with Nat's dad, didn't you?"

"Yes," answered Dave. "Did Nat tell you?" he added quickly.

"No, I know of the whole thing by accident. I had to go to the building where Mr. Poole has his new office. While I was waiting to see a man and deliver a message for my dad I overheard some talk between Mr. Poole and Nat. It was mighty warm, I can tell you!"

"What was said?" demanded Phil.

"Mr. Poole accused Nat of something and Nat, at first, denied it. Then Mr. Poole said something about arrest, and Professor Potts, and Nat got scared and begged his father to save him. Then Mr. Poole mentioned Dave and a pistol and said he couldn't do anything if that's the way matters stood, and Nat began to beg for dear life, asking his father to let Dave alone this time. At last Mr. Poole said he would, but the way he lectured Nat was a caution. He said he wouldn't give Nat a cent more of spending-money this summer."

"Hurrah, that lets you out, Dave!" cried Roger. "The case against you is squashed."

"The Pooles will have to let it drop," added the shipowner's son. "And I am mighty glad of it."

"I hope you are right," said Dave, and his face showed his relief.

They had to tell Ben all about what had happened. Then the latter wanted to see the bear target, and the crowd ended by doing some more target practicing. But this time Dave was very careful how he shot, and so were the others.

It had been decided that the start for the West was to be made early the following week, and for several days the boys and the girls were busy getting ready. Laura had traveled a great deal, so the journey would not be a novelty to her, but with Jessie it was different.

"I know I shall like it, once I am there," said Jessie. "But, oh, it seems such a distance to go!"

"We'll take good care of you," answered Dunston Porter.

"And I am sure you'll like Mrs. Endicott and Belle," added Laura. "Belle is as full of fun as a—a—oh, I don't know what."

"Shad is of bones," suggested Dave, who stood by.

"Oh, what a comparison!" cried Jessie, and then giggled in the regulation girl fashion.

They were to take a local train to Buffalo and change at that city for Chicago. Ben Basswood decided to go with them as far as Buffalo, so there would be quite a party. The boys gathered their things together and were ready to start a full day beforehand. The buying of railroad tickets and berths in the Pullmans was left entirely to Dunston Porter.

A farewell gathering had been arranged for the young people by Mrs. Wadsworth, to take place on the afternoon previous to their departure for the West. About a dozen boys and girls from Crumville and vicinity were invited. The party was held on the lawn of the Wadsworth estate, which was trimmed for the occasion with banners, flags, and lanterns. A small orchestra, located in the summerhouse, furnished the music.

Of course Dave and his chums donned their best for this occasion, and Laura and Jessie appeared in white dresses that were as pretty as they could be. Jessie's wavy hair was tied up in new ribbons, and as Dave looked at her he thought she looked as sweet as might a fairy from fairyland. He could not help smiling at her, and when she came and pinned on his coat a buttonhole bouquet he thought he was the happiest boy in the whole world.

"Oh, but won't we have the grand times when we get out West!" he said to her.

"I hope so, Dave," she answered. "But—"

"But what, Jessie?" he questioned, as he saw her hesitate.

"I—I can't get that Link Merwell out of my head. I am so sorry his father's ranch is next to that we are going to visit."

"Oh, don't worry. We'll make Link keep his distance," he returned, lightly. Yet it must be confessed that he was just a bit worried himself.

Among the first boys to arrive was Ben Basswood, and he lost no time in calling Phil and Roger aside.

"I don't want to worry Dave or the others," said Ben. "But I think somebody ought to be told."

"Told what?" asked the senator's son.

"About Nat Poole. I got the word from a friend of mine, Joe Devine. Joe was talking with Nat Poole, and he said Nat was very angry at all of us, and angry because Mrs. Wadsworth was giving us the party, especially as he wasn't invited. Joe said Nat intimated that he was going to make the affair turn out a fizzle."

"A fizzle?" queried Phil. "How?"

"Joe didn't know, but he told me, on the quiet, that I ought to watch out, and ought to warn the others. But I don't like to say anything to Mrs. Wadsworth, or the girls. You see, it may be only talk, and if it is, what's the use of getting the ladies excited?"

"It would be just like Nat to play some dirty trick," said the shipowner's son. "The question is, What will it be?"

"Somebody ought to stand guard," was Roger's advice. "And I think we ought to tell Dave."

This was readily agreed upon, and Dave was told a few minutes later. His face at once showed his concern.

"It mustn't be allowed!" he said, earnestly. "I don't care so much on my own account, but think of Mrs. Wadsworth and the girls! Yes, we must keep our eyes open, and if anything goes wrong—" He finished with a grave shake of his head.

"What are you boys plotting about?" asked Laura, as she came up. "Come, it won't do to stick together like this, with all the girls arriving. Dave, go and make folks at home,—and you do likewise," she added, with a smile at Phil and Roger.

The boys dispersed and mingled with the arriving guests. Dave did all he could to make everybody feel at home, but all the while he was doing it he kept his eyes wide open.

Presently, chancing to look in the direction of the automobile house, Dave saw somebody skulking along a hedge. The person was visible only a second, so the youth could not make out who it was.

"Maybe it's all right, but I'll take a look and make sure," he told himself, and excused himself to a girl to whom he had been talking. As he hurried across the lawn he passed Phil.

"Come with me, will you?" he said, in a low voice.

"See anything?" demanded the shipowner's son.

"I saw somebody, but I am not sure who it was."

Taking care not to make his departure noticeable, Dave walked toward the automobile house and Phil followed him. Soon the pair were behind some rose bushes and then they gained the shelter of the heavy hedge.

"There he is!" said Dave, in a low voice. "It's Nat Poole, sure enough!"

"What's he doing?" asked Phil.

"Nothing just now. But I guess he is up to something."

Keeping well out of sight behind the hedge, the two boys watched the son of the money-lender. Nat was sneaking past the automobile house and making for a washing-shed adjoining the kitchen of the mansion.

"I think I know what he is up to," murmured Dave. "Come on after him, Phil."

As silently as shadows Dave and Phil followed the money-lender's son to the shed. Once Nat looked around to see if the coast was clear, and the followers promptly dropped down behind a lilac bush. Reassured, Nat entered the shed, and Dave and Phil tiptoed their way up and got behind the open door.

The hired help were in the kitchen, so the shed was empty. On the floor stood an ice-cream freezer full of home-made ice-cream, and on a shelf rested several freshly baked cakes, all covered with chocolate icing, set out to harden.

"Now I'll fix things," Dave and Phil heard the money-lender's son mutter. "Salt in the cream and salt in the layer cakes will do the trick! Some of the boys and girls will think they are poisoned!"

Nat took up a bag of salt that was handy,—used for making the cream,—and proceeded to open the can in the freezer. Dave watched him as a cat does a mouse.

Just as Nat was on the point of dumping some of the salt into the ice-cream he felt himself jerked backwards. The salt dropped to the floor, and Nat found himself confronting Dave, with Phil but a few steps away.

"You contemptible rascal!" cried Dave, his eyes flashing.

"Why—I—er—" stammered the money-lender's son. He did not know what to say.

"Going to spoil the cream, eh?" came from Phil. "It was a mighty dirty trick, Nat."

"On a level with what you did to Professor Potts," added Dave.

"I—er—I wasn't going to do nothing!" cried Nat, with little regard for grammar. "I—er—I was looking at the ice-cream, that's all."

"A poor excuse is worse than none," answered Dave, grimly. "You were going to put salt in the cream and spoil it, you needn't deny it."

"See here, Dave Porter, I want you to understand—"

"Don't talk, Nat, we know all about it," broke in Phil. "You planned to come here yesterday, and we can prove it. We were on the lookout for you."

At this assertion the face of the money-lender's son changed. He grew quite pale.

"I haven't time to waste on you—I want to enjoy this party," said Dave. "Come along with me."

"Where to?" demanded Nat.

"I'll show you," answered Dave, and caught the money-lender's son by the arm. "Catch hold of him, Phil, and don't let him escape."

Edward Stratemeyer

CHAPTER V

AT NIAGARA FALLS

"See here, I want you to let me alone!" stormed Nat Poole, and he tried to jerk himself free.

"Listen, Nat," said Dave, sternly. "If you make a noise it will be the worse for you, for it will bring the others here, and then we'll tell about what you tried to do. Maybe Mrs. Wadsworth will call an officer, and anyway all the girls and the boys will be down on you. Now, if you want Phil and me to keep this a secret, you've got to come along with us."

"Where to?" grumbled Nat, doggedly.

"You'll soon see," returned Dave, briefly, and with a wink at his chum.

Somewhat against his will, Nat walked toward the end of the garden. He wished to escape from Mrs. Wadsworth and the others, but he was afraid Dave and Phil contemplated doing something disagreeable to him. Maybe they would give him a sound thrashing.

"Don't you touch me—don't you dare!" he cried, when the barn was readied. "Remember, my father can have you locked up, Dave Porter!"

"Well, don't forget what Professor Potts can do to you, Nat," answered Dave.

"What are you going to do?" asked Phil, in an aside to his chum.

Dave was trying to think. He had been half of a mind to lock Nat in the harness closet until the party was over—thus preventing him from making more trouble. Now, however, as he heard a locomotive whistle, a new thought struck him.

"Come on down to the railroad tracks, Nat," he said.

"What for?"

"Maybe you can take a journey for your health—if the freight train stops at the water tank."

"I—er—I don't understand."

"You will—if the train stops—and I think it will."

The three boys pushed off across the fields to where the railroad tracks were located. Here was the very spot where Dave had been picked up years before. Not far off was a water tank, where the locomotives usually stopped for their supply. A long freight train was just slowing down. Many of the cars were empty and the doors stood wide open.

"Up you go, Nat!" cried Dave.

"Me? Where?"

"Into one of the empty cars. You are going to have a ride for your health."

"Not much! Why, that train don't stop short of Jack's Junction, twelve miles from here!"

"I know it. You can walk back—the exercise will do

you good."

"I—er—I don't want to go!" And Nat made as if to run away. But Dave and Phil held him.

"But you are going!" cried Dave. "In you go!"

He and Phil forced the money-lender's son toward one of the open cars. Still protesting, Nat was shoved up and through one of the open doors. The door on the other side was closed. He ran to it, but found it locked from the outside.

"Hi, you let me off!" he cried, as the train gave a jerk and commenced to move.

"Don't jump, you might hurt yourself!" cried Dave, and shoved the door shut.

"Hope you have a pleasant journey!" called out Phil, merrily.

"And a nice walk back!" added Dave.

The freight train quickly gathered headway. Dave and Phil ran down by the side of the tracks. They saw Nat shove back the door about a foot and peer out. He did not dare to jump, and, seeing them, shook his fist wildly.

"He's off!" cried the shipowner's son, and then commenced to laugh. "Dave, that was just all right! He's booked for quite a journey."

"Twelve miles, or more, and he'll either have to wait for a train, and pay his fare back, or walk."

"Exactly. And if the train hands catch him, maybe they'll give him the thrashing he deserves."

"They'll hustle him off pretty lively, that's sure. Well, one thing is certain, he won't bother this party any more," added

Dave. "Let us get back."

They hurried to the house, and as they did so the freight train passed out of sight and hearing. They thought they had seen the last of Nat, but they were mistaken.

"Where have you boys been?" asked Laura, when they reappeared, after having brushed off their clothing.

"I'll tell you later," answered her brother.

"Anything serious?"

"Not very. It's all over now, Laura."

The party was now in full swing and proved a big success. The boys and girls played all sorts of games, and also did a little dancing. Then refreshments were served. When the ice cream and cake were passed around, Phil and Dave could not help but look at each other, and the shipowner's son winked suggestively.

"Why are you winking at Dave?" demanded Roger.

"Did I wink?" questioned Phil, solemnly, and then Dave began to laugh and almost choked on a piece of cake in his mouth.

After the refreshments came more games and some singing, and it was nine o'clock before the lawn party came to an end. The girls and boys from the town went home mostly in pairs, but Ben remained behind, for he knew Dave and Phil had something to tell. All the lads congregated in the summerhouse and Laura and Jessie went with them.

"Wanted to spoil the ice-cream and chocolate layer-cakes!" cried Jessie. "Oh, how mean!"

"It served him right, to put him on the freight train!" was Laura's comment. "I hope he was carried about fifty miles, and has to walk back."

"He'll be trying another trick before we leave," said Roger. "We must keep our eyes open."

"Isn't it a shame he can't be nice?" came from Jessie. "If he keeps on like this, he'll not have a friend in the world."

"Well, he hasn't many friends now," answered Dave. "At Oak Hall the majority of the fellows turned him down just as they turned down Link Merwell."

"Oh, that Link Merwell!" sighed Laura. "I trust I never see or hear of him again!"

Bright and early the next day the boys arose and packed the last of their baggage. The girls were up, too, and joined the lads at the breakfast table. Dave's father was there, and also Uncle Dunston, as well as Mr. and Mrs. Wadsworth.

"Well, I certainly hope you all have a grand time," said the rich manufacturer.

"And I hope the outing does Jessie good," said his wife. Jessie was not very strong and the doctor had said that a trip to the Far West might do much towards building up her constitution.

"You must write often," said Mr. Porter to his daughter. "And make Dave write, too."

"I'll not forget," said the daughter, and Dave nodded.

It was rather a sober meal, although every one tried to be cheerful. The big touring-car, Mr. Wadsworth's latest purchase, was at the door, and the baggage had gone on ahead. Soon it was time to go.

"Good-by, everybody!" cried Dave, and shook hands with his

father and Mrs. and Mr. Wadsworth. The lady of the house gave him a warm kiss, and kissed all the others.

"Wish you were going too, daddy!" cried Laura to her father.

"Well, I'll go the next time," was the answer, with a smile.

In another five minutes the boys and girls and Dunston Porter were off for the depot, the others waving their hands as the travelers disappeared. Tears came to Mrs. Wadsworth's eyes, at the parting with Jessie, yet she did her best to smile.

"We'll be back in six weeks!" called out Dave. "And as brown as berries and as strong as oxen!" And this caused everybody to laugh. Little did any of them realize what adventures those six weeks were to contain.

The train for Buffalo was on time, and when it rolled into the station they climbed on board, and the boys found the right seats in the parlor car and settled the girls. Ben was there, and had a seat with the crowd.

"I've got news," said Ben, as the train went on its way. "Nat Poole isn't back yet."

"Who told you?"

"Tom Marvin. He called this morning to see Nat about something. Nat had sent a telegram home from a place called Halock, stating he had been carried off on a freight train."

"Humph! then he went further than we supposed he would," mused Phil. "Where is Halock?"

Nobody knew, and they consulted a time-table taken from a rack in the car.

"It's a flag-station not far from Buffalo," announced Roger. "Say, he certainly was carried some distance!"

Edward Stratemeyer

"What if he didn't have any money to get home with?" asked Laura.

"Maybe he telegraphed for some," said Phil.

"He could pawn his watch—he always wears one," added Ben. "But it is queer that he didn't get off at Jack's Junction."

"Perhaps he liked to ride—after he once got used to it," returned the senator's son.

On and on went the train, stopping at several towns of more or less importance. The girls and boys amused themselves studying the time-table and in gazing out of the window, and Dunston Porter told them of some of his experiences while roving in various portions of the globe, for, as my old readers are aware, he was a great traveler. At noon they went into the dining-car for lunch, and Dave and Roger sat at one table with Laura and Jessie opposite to them.

"Say, this puts me in mind of a story, as Shadow Hamilton would say," said the senator's son, as the train rushed along while they ate. "A little girl had a sandwich on a train like this, once, and then boasted afterwards that she had eaten a sandwich three miles long."

"Well, I think I'll eat some roast beef ten miles long," said Dave. "And two miles of apple pie to boot!" And this caused the girls to giggle.

They reached Buffalo in the middle of the afternoon and there had to wait until half-past ten for the night express to Chicago. Here Ben left them, for the boat he was to take was waiting at the dock.

"Send me a letter to Duluth," he said, on parting, and Dave promised to do so.

"I'll tell you what we might do," said Dunston Porter. "We

can take a trolley trip to Niagara Falls and come back on a train. We have plenty of time."

"Oh, yes, I'd like to see Niagara!" cried Jessie, clapping her hands.

The others all voted the suggestion a good one, and soon, having checked their baggage at the depot, they boarded a trolley car bound for the Falls.

"We can look at the Falls for an hour, get supper, and still have time in which to return to Buffalo," said Mr. Porter. "When we get there we can get a carriage to drive us around."

The trolley car made good time and it was still daylight when Niagara was reached. Hackmen were numerous, and Dunston Porter soon engaged a turnout to take them around Goat Island and other points of interest. They could hear the roaring of the Falls plainly, and the sight of the great cataracts impressed them deeply. "Want to go down under the Falls?" asked Phil, as they were riding along.

"No, indeed!" answered Laura.

"We haven't time, anyway," answered Roger. "We've got to get back or we'll miss that train for Chicago, and that won't do, for our berths have been engaged ahead."

At the bridge leading to the Three Sisters Islands the whole party alighted, so as to get a better view of the upper rapids of the river. As they did so, a youth seated on a rock near by looked at them in amazement. Then of a sudden he slipped off the rock and dodged out of sight.

The youth was Nat Poole.

Edward Stratemeyer

CHAPTER VI

NAT POOLE'S LITTLE GAME

It may not be out of place here to relate how Nat Poole happened to be at Niagara Falls, and how he chanced to have with him a man who was willing to do almost anything for the sake of a little money.

When Nat was placed aboard of the freight train by Dave and Phil he was in a great rage, yet powerless, for the time being, to help himself. The train moved so swiftly that he did not dare to jump off, and soon Crumville was left far behind.

As soon as he had cooled off for a little, Nat found out that he was very tired. He had been out the night before with some of the fast young men of the town, playing cards and pool, and had had but two hours' sleep in twenty-four. He found a pile of old bagging in one end of the freight car and sat down to rest. Presently his eyes closed, and before he knew it he was sound asleep. He continued to sleep during the stop at Jack's Junction, and he did not notice another party enter the freight car, nor did he notice the door being closed and locked.

When Nat awoke it was with a sense of pain. The other party in the car had stepped on his ankle. He gave a cry and this was answered by an exclamation of astonishment.

"Who are you?" asked Nat, sitting up and then leaping to his feet.

"I reckon I can ask the same question," returned the stranger.

"Are you a train hand?"

"Are you?"

"No."

"Neither am I."

There was a moment of silence after this, and then the unknown lit a match and held it close to Nat. Both gave a cry of astonishment.

"Hello! You are Nat Poole, the boy I met at Rally's Pool Parlors," said the stranger.

"Yes, and you are Tom Shocker, the traveling salesman."

"Right you are—but I'm not a traveling salesman any longer," answered Tom Shocker, and gave a short laugh.

"Why?" asked Nat.

"Lost my job."

"I suppose your boss found out that you were spending your time playing cards and pool," said Nat. "How did you make out after I left you?"

"Lost all I had. That's the reason I am stealing a ride on this freight," answered the man. "But what are you doing here?" he continued in curiosity.

In his own fashion Nat related how he had been attacked by two of his former school enemies, dragged to the car and thrown in. He added that he had been next to unconscious, and so was unable to fight off Dave and Phil. Then he asked how Tom Shocker happened to be on board.

"I got on at Jack's Junction," said the man. "I haven't got but fifty cents left and I thought I'd beat my way to Buffalo, where I think I can get some more cash. But I didn't think they'd lock the door of the car."

During the ride to Halock, Tom Shocker managed to learn a good deal about Nat and his trouble with Dave and the others, and he also learned that the youth had considerable spending-money with him. The car was opened at Halock and run off on a siding, and the pair got off.

"Let us take a trolley to Buffalo," said Shocker. "There we can get a room at a hotel—that is, if you'll put up the price."

"All right; I might as well go to Buffalo, now I am so close," answered Nat. "But I'll send word home first," he added, and this was done.

After resting at a hotel in Buffalo, Tom Shocker proposed a trip to Niagara Falls, Nat, of course, to pay the way.

"I'll pay you back some day," said Shocker, offhandedly. "When I strike another situation I'll have plenty of cash. And, in the meantime, if you want me to do anything for you, say the word. I am open for any proposition that you may offer."

On the way to the Falls, Tom Shocker told much about himself, and Nat learned that the fellow was one of those shiftless mortals who change from one situation to another. He had been a salesman on the road for five different concerns, had run a restaurant, a poolroom, and a moving-picture show, and had even been connected with a prize-fighting affair. He did not care what he did so long a it paid, and many of his transactions had been of the shady sort.

Nat did not enjoy the visit to the Falls as much as he had anticipated. He found Tom Shocker rather coarse, and the man wanted to drink whenever the opportunity afforded. From the rapids below the Falls the pair walked to Goat

Island, and there Nat was on the point of giving Shocker the slip when he chanced to see Dave and the others of the party.

"What's the matter?" demanded Shocker, who stood close by, as he saw the money-lender's son dart out of sight behind the rocks.

"Do you see that boy?" demanded Nat, pointing with his hand.

"Yes."

"That is Dave Porter, the fellow who put me on the freight car. And over yonder is Phil Lawrence, the other chap."

"You don't say! What brings them here?"

"They are on their way out West, and I suppose they ran up here to see the sights. I—I wish I could do something to 'em!" added Nat, bitterly.

"Maybe you can," answered Tom Shocker, always open for action. "I'll tell you one thing," he continued, in a low tone. "If they had treated me as they treated you, I'd not let them off so easily."

"Will you help me, if I—er—try to fix that Dave Porter?" asked Nat. "He started it. I don't care so much about Lawrence."

"Sure I'll help you. Anything you say goes," answered Tom Shocker, readily. He thought he saw a chance of getting another dollar or two out of Nat.

The two walked behind some bushes and there talked the matter over for several minutes.

"Fargo's is the place to go to," said Shocker, presently. "I know we can trust him."

"Of course, I don't want to hurt Porter," said Nat, nervously. "I only want to scare him."

"Sure, I understand. We'll scare the wits out of him," returned Tom Shocker. "Now, let me see. I have it—we'll catch him on the bridge. His carriage is bound to come that way, to get off Goat Island."

Dave and his friends spent the best part of a quarter of an hour around the Three Sisters Islands and then returned to their carriage.

"Now we can go to the hotel and have dinner," said Dunston Porter. "And then we can take a local train back to Buffalo."

The carriage was just crossing the bridge that connects Goat Island with the city of Niagara Falls when a man stepped up and stopped the turnout. It was Tom Shocker.

"Excuse me, but I reckon this is the number, 176," he said. "Is there a young man here named David Porter?"

"Yes, I am Dave Porter," answered Dave, and looked at Shocker curiously. The fellow was a total stranger to him.

"Got a note for you," went on Shocker, and produced it. It was sealed and marked *Private* in plain letters.

Wondering what the note could contain, Dave opened and read it. His face changed color and he gave a little gasp.

"Excuse me, I'll have to—to leave you for a little while," he stammered to the others.

"What's the matter?" asked Roger.

"I—I can't tell you just now." Dave turned to his uncle. "Where will you get dinner, Uncle Dunston?"

"At the International."

"All right—I'll be there before long," answered Dave, and sprang to the ground.

"But what's up?" cried Phil. He could see that his chum was much disturbed.

"I—I can't tell you, Phil. But I'll be back before you finish your dinner."

"Don't you want some one along?" asked Laura, who did not like to see her brother depart in the company of such a looking stranger as Tom Shocker.

"No, Laura. Oh, it's all right. I'll be at the International on time," said Dave, and then he hurried over the bridge and down a side street of the city, in company with Tom Shocker.

The note Dave had received was written in a cramped hand and ran as follows:

> "DEAR DAVE:—You will be surprised to receive this, but I saw you in town to-day and noted the number of your carriage. I am in deep trouble and would like you to come and see me in private, if only for five or ten minutes. You can aid me a great deal. Please don't tell any of the others of your party. The man who brings this to you will take you to me. Please, *please* don't disappoint me.
>
> "Yours truly,
> "ANDREW DALE."

Andrew Dale was the first assistant teacher at Oak Hall, and an instructor who had made himself very dear to Dave and some of the other boys. He had sided with Dave when the latter was termed "a poorhouse nobody," and this had made teacher and pupil close friends.

"What's the matter with my friend?" asked Dave, as he and Tom Shocker hurried through several side streets of the city.

"I don't know exactly," was the reply. "Money matters, I think, and the gent is sick, too. He wanted it kept very quiet—said it might ruin his reputation if it got out."

"Well, I didn't say anything to anybody," answered Dave. "How much further have we to go?"

"Only a couple of blocks."

But the "couple of blocks" proved to be five, and they had to make another turn or two. Then they came to the side door of a building used as a lodging house and a pool and billiard parlor. This resort was run by a man named Bill Fargo, a sport who had once had dealings with Shocker in a prize-fighting enterprise.

"He's got a room here—up on the third floor," said Shocker, as he saw Dave hesitate. "Come on, I'll show you."

He went ahead, up the somewhat dilapidated stairs, and Dave followed. In the pool and billiard parlors below some men were laughing and talking, and clicking the ivory balls together, but upstairs it was silent, and nobody seemed to be around.

During the past few years of his life Dave had had a number of stirring adventures, and he was by no means as green as he had been when first he had set out for Oak Hall. He did not like the looks of his surroundings, and he resolved to keep his wits about him and be on his guard.

"Why should Mr. Dale come to a place like this?" he asked himself. He knew the teacher to be a model man, who did not drink or gamble.

"Here we are," said Tom Shocker, as he stopped in front of a door at the back of the hallway on the third floor of the building. "I guess you can go right in. He's on the bed with his broken ankle."

"His broken ankle?" repeated Dave. "Why didn't you tell me of that before?"

"I thought I did," returned Shocker, smoothly. "Here you are. It's dark, isn't it? I'll light the gas," and he commenced to fumble in his pocket, as if hunting for a match.

It was dark, and for several seconds Dave could see little or nothing. He heard a faint groan.

"Is that you, Mr. Dale?" he asked, kindly.

A low reply was returned—so low that Dave could not make out what was said. He went into the room a few steps further. As he did so Tom Shocker closed the door and locked it. Dave heard the click of the lock's bolt and wheeled around.

"What did you do?" he demanded sharply.

"I guess I've got you now, Dave Porter!" cried another voice, and now Dave recognized the tones of Nat Poole. "You played me a scurvy trick by putting me aboard the freight train. I guess it's about time I paid you back; don't you think so?"

CHAPTER VII

IN WHICH DAVE IS ROBBED

Dave found himself in a decidedly unpleasant situation. The door of the room was locked and Tom Shocker stood against it. The man lit the gas, but allowed it to remain low. Dave saw Nat Poole standing close to a bed. The money-lender's son had a small bottle and some cotton in his hand.

"I suppose this is a trick?" said Dave, as coolly as he could.

"Rather good one, too, isn't it?" returned Nat, lightly.

"That depends on how you look at it, Nat. Did you forge Mr. Dale's name?"

"Why—er—I—er—"

"That isn't a nice business to be in."

"Humph! you needn't preach to me, Dave Porter! You played a dirty trick on me and I am going to pay you back."

"What are you going to do?"

"You'll see soon enough."

"I want you to open that door!" cried Dave, wheeling around and confronting Tom Shocker. "Open it at once!"

"This is none of my affair, Mr. Porter," answered the man, with a slight sneer. "You can settle it with Mr. Poole."

"I'll settle with you, you rascal!" cried Dave, and leaping forward he caught Tom Shocker by the shoulder and forced him aside. "Give me that key!"

"Don't you do it!" cried Nat. "Here, wait, I'll fix him! Hold him!"

Nat poured some of the stuff in the bottle on the cotton and advanced on Dave. At the same time Tom Shocker caught Dave by both arms and essayed to hold him.

Dave was strong, and a sudden fear gave him additional strength. He might have been a match for his two assailants, but for the stuff on the cotton. This was chloroform, and when Nat clapped the saturated cotton to his mouth and nose he was speedily rendered all but unconscious.

"Don't give him too much!" he heard Tom Shocker say.

"You watch him, while I tie his hands," answered Nat, and then Dave was forced back and onto the bed. He struggled weakly, but could not free himself, and before he realized it he was a close prisoner, with his hands tied fast to the head of the bed and his feet fast to the lower end. He was flat on his back.

"Now, you can stay there until somebody comes to release you," said Nat, mockingly. "I reckon that will teach you a lesson not to send me off on freight trains!"

"Nat, I've got to get back to Buffalo to catch my train for Chicago."

"Humph. Not to-night. You'll stay here."

"The others will worry about me."

"Let them worry. I'll be glad of it."

"Better destroy that note," suggested Tom Shocker. Then he noticed Dave's watch and chain, and valuable stickpin, and his eyes glistened. He began to wonder how much money the lad had in his pocket.

The note was taken by Nat. Then the money-lender's son took a soft pillow and placed it over Dave's face.

"That will keep you from calling too loudly," he said. "I guess it won't hurt your breathing though. Come," he added to the man. "Let us get out of here, before somebody comes."

"All right," answered Tom Shocker. He gazed wistfully at Dave's watchchain and at the stickpin. "I—er—all right," he added, and followed Nat to the door.

The pair walked outside and the man locked the door. Then both hurried below and out of the side door to the street. They went as far as the corner.

"Let us make for the depot," said Nat, who was plainly nervous. Now that the trick had been played he was becoming alarmed over the possible consequences. "You don't think he'll smother?" he asked, anxiously.

"Smother? Not a bit of it," answered Tom Shocker. "He'll be out of that room inside of an hour. He wasn't tied very hard, and he's sure to make a racket sooner or later."

Tom Shocker went with Nat a distance of two blocks more and then came to a sudden halt.

"By jove, I forgot!" he cried. "I must see my old friend, Dickson, before I leave town. It won't take me but a few minutes. You go to the depot and wait for me." And before the money-lender's son could reply, he was off, down another side street.

Tom Shocker was well acquainted with the thoroughfares of Niagara Falls and it did not take him long to double on his tracks and return to Fargo's resort. He mounted the stairs, pulling his hat far down over his forehead as he did so. Then he tied his handkerchief over the lower portion of his face. He had the key of the room still in his possession, and with it he unlocked the door.

The light was still burning, and on the bed he could see Dave struggling to free himself of his bonds and of the pillow which still rested lightly over his head. Holding the pillow in place with one hand Shocker gained possession of the watch and chain and stickpin with the other. Then he took from Dave's pocket a small roll of bank-bills. He tried to appropriate the lad's ring, but could not get it off the finger.

Dave, finding himself being robbed, struggled harder than ever. But the bonds held and he was helpless to protect himself. In less than two minutes Tom Shocker accomplished his purpose, and then he glided out of the room silently, once more locking the door. Once on the street he set off on a brisk walk, but he did not go in the direction of the depot.

"I reckon I can afford to part company with Poole now," the man told himself. "Won't there be a row when that Porter gets free! But he can't blame me!" he added, with a chuckle.

Left once more to himself, Dave continued to struggle, and at last he managed to toss the pillow from his face. Then he breathed more freely, for which he was thankful.

"What a mean trick!" he murmured, as he saw that his watch was gone.

Presently he heard footsteps passing along the hallway, and he uttered a call. The footsteps came to a stop.

"Come in here, please!" he called. "I need help."

Edward Stratemeyer

"What's up?" asked somebody outside, and then the door was tried. Soon a key was inserted in the lock, the door was opened, and a chambermaid showed herself.

"Untie me at once!" cried Dave.

The maid turned up the gas and then uttered a cry of astonishment. Without waiting to question the youth she flew out of the room and down the stairs, to return, a few minutes later, with a burly man.

"What's this mean?" asked the man, as he commenced to untie the ropes that held Dave.

"It's a trick that was played on me," answered Dave, thinking rapidly. He was on the point of stating that he had been robbed, but he did not wish to create too much of a scene. He felt sure that Nat would, sooner or later, return his belongings to him.

"A trick, eh?" said the hotel proprietor. "Certainly a queer one. Where are the fellows who hired this room?"

"I don't know. They tied me fast and left."

"Did you know them?"

"I knew one of them—he goes to boarding school with me."

"Oh, I see, a schoolboy's trick, eh? You schoolboys are up to all sorts of pranks."

"You don't know where they went to, do you?" questioned Dave, as he leaped up from the bed and stretched himself.

"No, I haven't the least idea. They hired this room for to-night, that's all."

"I think I'll try to catch them," said the youth. "Much obliged for setting me free."

"You are welcome. But say, I don't want any more skylarking around here," added the proprietor of the resort, as Dave hurried out of the room and down the stairs.

He had found his hat on the floor, and, after brushing up a little, he started on a brisk walk for the hotel where the others were to have dinner. He did not, of course, know the way, and so hired a newsboy for a dime to act as guide.

"Dave! you have been away a long time!" cried Laura, as he appeared. "We have almost finished eating."

"Never mind, I can get all I wish in a few minutes," he answered.

"Why, your stickpin is gone!" cried Jessie. "And your watch-chain, too."

"Dave, have you been robbed?" questioned his uncle, quickly.

"Yes and no," he answered, with a grim smile. "I suppose I might as well tell you what happened," he continued, and then gave a few of the details. Then he had to tell his uncle how Nat had been put aboard the freight car.

"Well, it's a case of tit for tat, I suppose," said Dunston Porter. "You can thank your stars that you got away so quickly. A little later and you would have missed the train,—and we would have missed it, too—for I should not have gone on without you."

"I suppose Nat thinks he has the laugh on you," said Roger. "But what of your watch and pin and money? Are you going West without them?"

"I suppose I'll have to. But I'll make him give them up in short order. I'll send him a telegram."

"Tell him if he doesn't send them on by express at once that you will put the case in the hands of the law," said Phil. "That will scare him."

Dave was quickly served with a meal, and he lost no time in eating what he wanted. Then the entire party walked toward the railroad station, to catch the train for Buffalo.

"I was a chump to follow that man up into that room," said Dave to his chums. "Next time I'll be more on my guard. But I thought Mr. Dale must be in some dire trouble."

"It was a nervy thing to do—to forge his name," was the comment of the senator's son. "It's a pity you didn't keep the note."

"I couldn't. After I was tied up they had me at their mercy."

"Who was the man?"

"I don't know. I never saw him before."

"He must have been some friend of Nat's."

"I suppose so."

Arriving at the station, they found they had several minutes to wait. When the train rolled in all got on board but Roger, who was buying a late newspaper from a boy on the platform.

"Hurry up, or you'll get left!" cried Dave.

"I'll get on the car behind!" cried the senator's son, and did so. He did not rejoin his companions until the train was on its way towards Buffalo.

"What do you think!" he cried. "Nat Poole is on board!"

"Nat!" ejaculated Dave. "Is that man with him?"

"No, Nat seems to be alone."

"Did he see you?"

"I don't think so. He was crouched down in a seat, as if in deep thought."

"I'll interview him," said Dave, and left the car, followed by Phil, Roger, and his uncle.

"Don't quarrel on the train," cautioned Dunston Porter. "But insist upon it that Nat return your belongings."

Roger readily led the way to where the son of the Crumville money-lender sat, crouched down, and with his eyes partly closed. When touched on the shoulder Nat sat up, and a look of fright came into his face.

"Why—er—why—" he stammered and was unable to proceed.

"Didn't expect to see me quite so soon, did you?" returned Dave, pleasantly, and dropped into the seat beside him. "Nat, if it's all the same to you, I'll take my watch, my stickpin, and my money," he added, coldly.

"Your what?" exclaimed Nat. Then he stared blankly at Dave. "I—er—I don't understand you."

"Yes, you do. I want my things, and I want them at once!"

"I haven't got your things, and you needn't say I have!" retorted the money-lender's son. "Oh, I see how it is," he added, struck by a sudden thought. "You want to play another joke on me, don't you? Well, it won't work this time. I didn't touch your things, and you know it."

CHAPTER VIII

THE YOUTH IN THE BALCONY

For a moment Dave stared at Nat Poole in perplexity. He saw that the money-lender's son was in earnest. Like a flash he realized that something was wrong.

"See here, I want no more fooling, Nat," he said, sharply. "My watch and chain, my scarfpin, and thirty-three dollars in bills were taken from me, either by you or your companion. I want them back, and now!"

"Dave, you—er—you don't mean that you—you were—robbed?" Nat could hardly utter the words. His teeth were fairly chattering with sudden fright.

"I certainly was, if you want to call it by such an ugly name."

"But I didn't touch the things, you know I didn't!"

"Then your companion did."

"No, he didn't, he came away with me, you know that. All we did was to tie you fast and throw that pillow over your face. Then we came away and locked the door. It was only a bit of fun, to pay you back for putting me on the freight car."

"One of you came back and took the things. I couldn't see who it was, for the pillow was still over my head."

"I didn't come back—I give you my word of honor. Shocker must have done it! Oh, the rascal!" And now Nat's face showed his concern.

"Who was that man?" asked the senator's son.

"A fellow I met in Crumville a few days ago. He appeared to be straight enough." And then Nat told his story from beginning to end. He said that he had hung around the depot waiting for Tom Shocker to come, but that the fellow had failed to show himself.

"It's as plain as day," said Phil. "If Nat's story is true, this Shocker went back and robbed Dave."

"Yes, but if he did, Nat is partly responsible, for he left me tied up," said Dave.

"Of course he is responsible," came from Roger.

"I don't see how," grumbled the money-lender's son, but his uneasiness showed that he thought as did the others.

"You'll see how, if that Shocker doesn't show up with my things," said Dave, sternly. "I'll hold you and your father responsible for every dollar's worth."

This threat almost caused Nat to collapse, and he felt even worse when Dave added that the scarfpin and the watch and chain were worth about one hundred dollars.

"I'm going to hunt up Shocker's address as soon as I get home," said Nat. "I'll run him down, see if I don't—and I'll make him give the things up, too!"

"Well, I'll give you a fair amount of time," answered Dave. "After that I'll look to you and your father to make good."

Fortunately for Dave, he could easily get along without the

watch and the scarfpin, and his uncle let him have some money in place of that taken. But Mr. Porter told Nat that his father would have to settle the matter if Tom Shocker was not brought to book.

At Buffalo the others separated from Nat Poole, who said he was going to take the early morning train home. Nat felt very bad over the outcome of his joke, and to a certain extent Dave and his chums felt sorry for him.

"I was a big fool to take up with a stranger like Shocker," said the money-lender's son. "You'll not catch me doing it again! I only hope I can lay my hands on him!" Then, just as he was about to leave, he turned back and beckoned Dave to step to one side.

"What do you want now?" asked Dave.

"I want to show you that I—er—that is, I am not the enemy you think, Dave," was the low answer. "I am going to give you a warning. I wasn't going to say anything, at first. It's about a letter I got from Link Merwell."

"Merwell?" And now Dave was all attention.

"Yes, he sent it to me from Chicago, where he is stopping on his way to his father's ranch. He said he had heard that you were going to the Endicott ranch, and he added that if you came out West he would see to it that you got all that was coming to you—those are his very words."

"When did you get this letter?"

"A couple of days ago. Take my advice and beware of him, for he means business. When he left Oak Hall he was the maddest boy I ever saw. He will do something awful to you if he gets the chance."

"I'll be on my guard—and I am much obliged for telling me,"

said Dave; and then he and Nat separated, not to meet again for many weeks.

The train for Chicago was already standing in the station, and the Porters and their friends were soon on board. The two girls had a private compartment and the others several sections, and all proceeded to make themselves at home.

"I never get into a sleeping car without thinking of old Billy Dill, the sailor who went with me to the South Seas," said Dave to Laura and Jessie. "He thought we'd have to sleep in the seats, and when the porter came and made up the berths he was the most surprised man you ever saw."

"And where is he now?" asked Jessie.

"In a home for aged sailors. Father and Uncle Dunston have seen to it that he is comfortably cared for."

"I must visit him some day," said Laura. "Just think! if it hadn't been for him we might never have met, Dave!" And she gave her brother a tight hug.

The train was a comfortable one, and all of the party slept well. When they arose, they found themselves crossing the level stretches of Indiana. The boys and Mr. Porter took a good wash-up and were presently joined on the observation end of the car by Laura and Jessie.

"What a beautiful morning!" cried Jessie.

"I feel just as if I'd like to get out and walk," added Laura, and this caused the others to laugh.

They had an appetizing breakfast of fruit, fish, eggs, and rolls, with coffee, and took their time over the repast. Then Dunston Porter pointed out to them various points of interest. Before long, they reached a small town and then came to the suburbs of the great city by the lakes.

Edward Stratemeyer

"Here we are!" cried Roger, at last, as they ran into the immense train shed. Here all was bustle and seeming confusion, and they picked their way through the crowd with difficulty. The boys rather enjoyed this, but it made Laura and Jessie shrink back.

"Why, it's as bad as New York!" said Jessie.

"Almost," answered Dunston Porter. "Come, we'll soon find a couple of carriages to take us to the hotel."

That the girls and the others might see something of Chicago, it had been arranged to remain in that city two days. They were to stop at a new and elegant hotel on the lake shore, and thither they were driven with their baggage.

"It certainly is as bustling as New York," was Roger's comment, as they drove along. "Just look at the carriages, and autos, and trucks!"

"This afternoon we'll hire an automobile to take us around," said Dunston Porter. "It is the only way to see a good deal in a little time."

They were fortunate in getting good accommodations at the new hotel, and the boys and girls were struck by the elegance of the rooms, and, later, by the sumptuousness of the dining-hall.

"Why, it's fit for a palace!" declared Jessie.

"Beats the Crumville Hotel, doesn't it?" said Dave, dryly, and this caused the girls to giggle and the other boys to laugh.

An automobile was engaged at the stand in the hotel, and immediately after lunch the whole party went sightseeing, visiting the lake front, Lincoln Park, and numerous other points of interest. At the park they alighted to look at the animals, and this pleased the girls especially.

"To-morrow morning I'll have a little business to attend to," said Dunston Porter, "and I'll have to let you take care of yourselves for a few hours. I propose that you boys take the girls around to some of the big department stores."

"Oh, yes!" cried Laura, who had a woman's delight for finery. Jessie was also interested, for her opportunities for visiting big stores were rare.

Mr. Porter had already purchased tickets for one of the theaters, where they were playing a well-known and highly successful comedy drama, and this they attended that evening after dinner at the hotel. Their seats were on the right in the orchestra, so they had more or less of a chance to view the opposite side of the auditorium.

"They certainly have a full house," said Roger, who sat on one side of Dave, while Jessie sat on the other. "I believe every seat is taken."

"That shows that a good drama pays," answered Dave. "This is clean as well as interesting." His eyes were roving over the sea of faces, upstairs and down. "I wonder how many a theater like this can hold?"

"Two thousand, perhaps."

"It certainly looks it, Roger. That gallery—Well, I declare!"

"What is it?" asked the senator's son.

"Do you see that fellow in the front row in the balcony? The one next to the aisle?"

"Yes. What of him?"

"Looks to me like Link Merwell."

"Oh, Dave, you must be mistaken."

"I don't think so. It looks like Merwell, and Nat Poole said he was in Chicago."

"So he did. Now you speak of it, he does look like Merwell. Wish we had an opera glass, we might make sure."

"I'll see if we can't borrow a glass," said Dave.

He looked around and saw that a lady directly in front of Jessie had a pair of glasses in her lap. He spoke to Jessie, and the girl asked the lady to lend her the glasses for a minute, and the favor was readily granted, for it was between the acts, and there was nothing on the stage to look at. Dave adjusted the glasses and turned them on the balcony.

"It's Merwell, right enough," he announced.

"Let me see," said the senator's son, and took the glasses from Dave. As he pointed them at the youth in the balcony, the latter looked down on Roger and those with him. He gave a start and then leaned forward.

"It's Merwell, and he sees us!" cried Roger.

"What's up?" asked Phil, who was some seats away.

"Link Merwell,—up in the balcony," answered Dave, and pointed with his finger. Phil turned in the direction, and as he did so, Link Merwell doubled up his fist and raised it in the air for an instant.

"Merwell, sure as you're born," said the shipowner's son. "And full of fight!"

"Oh, Dave, you mustn't quarrel here!" whispered Laura, who sat on the other side of Roger.

"We'll not quarrel here," answered her brother. "But I am glad I saw him," he added to his chums. "Now we can keep on our guard."

The play went on, and, for the time being, the boys and the girls paid no further attention to Link Merwell. Just as the final curtain was being lowered, Dave looked up toward the balcony.

"He has gone," he announced.

"Perhaps he was afraid we'd come after him," suggested Phil.

"Maybe he came downstairs to watch for us," added Roger. "Keep your eyes open when we go out."

They did as the senator's son suggested. They saw nothing of Merwell in the foyer, but came face to face with the former student of Oak Hall on the sidewalk. He glared at them, but then seeing Dunston Porter at Dave's side, slunk behind some other people, and disappeared from view.

"My, what an ugly look!" said Laura, with a shiver.

"He looked as if he wanted to eat somebody up," was Jessie's comment. "Oh, Dave, you must be careful!"

"I wish his father's ranch wasn't so close to Mr. Endicott's," continued Dave's sister. "I declare, the more I think of it, the more nervous it makes me!"

"Don't you worry, Laura, or you either, Jessie," answered Dave. "We'll take care of Link Merwell. If he tries any of his games, he'll get the worst of it—just as he got the worst of it at Oak Hall."

But though Dave spoke thus bravely, he was much disturbed himself. He could read human nature pretty closely, and that look in Merwell's face had showed him that the fellow meant to do harm at the first opportunity that was afforded.

Edward Stratemeyer

CHAPTER IX

ONLY A STREET WAIF

In the morning Dunston Porter left the hotel early, stating that he would not return until lunch time. The boys and girls took their time over their breakfast, and then started out for a tour of the big stores located on State Street.

Two hours were spent in a way that pleased Laura and Jessie greatly. The girls purchased several things, to be mailed to the folks left behind. Then all walked around to the post-office, both to see the building and to send the things away.

It was while the others were addressing their packages and also some picture postcards, that Dave saw a sight that interested him greatly. Near one of the doorways was a small and ragged newsboy with half a dozen papers under his arm. An older youth had him by the shoulder and was shaking him viciously.

"I say it was a five-dollar gold piece I gave you yesterday by mistake!" the older boy was saying. "I want it back."

"No, it wasn't, mister," the boy answered. "It was a cent, nothing but a cent."

"I know better, you little thief! Give me that gold piece, or I'll call a policeman." And again the big youth shook the ragged newsboy, causing the papers to fall to the sidewalk.

"Why, it's Link Merwell!" murmured Dave to himself, and he stepped in the direction of the pair who were disputing. Merwell had his back to Dave and did not see him.

"Are you going to give me my gold piece or not?" demanded Link Merwell, and now he gave the newsboy such a twist of the shoulder that the ragged lad cried out with pain.

"I don't know anything about your gold piece!" cried the boy for at least the tenth time. "Let me go, please, mister! I ain't no thief!"

"I'll twist your little neck off for you!" muttered Merwell, and was on the point of hitting the boy in the face when Dave stepped up behind him and caught his arm.

"Don't you know better than to hit a little chap like this, Merwell?" he demanded.

"Porter!" muttered the western youth, and his face took on a sour look. "Say, this ain't none of your affair!" he burst out. "You keep your hands off."

"Please don't let him hurt me!" pleaded the ragged newsboy. "I didn't do wrong, mister. I ain't seen no gold piece. He gave me a cent yesterday for a newspaper, that's all." And the boy looked imploringly at Dave.

"He's got a five-dollar gold piece of mine," cried Link Merwell. "I want it. And what's more, Dave Porter, I want you to keep your nose out of my business!" he added, fiercely.

"Merwell," answered Dave, as calmly as he could, "I have no desire to interfere in your business. But I am not going to stand by and see you abuse this boy, or anybody else. I know just the sort you are—a bully."

"Bah! Just because you had me expelled from Oak Hall you think you can do anything, don't you? Well, just wait till you

Edward Stratemeyer

get out West, that's all! I'll show you a thing or two you won't forget as long as you live!"

"Take care that you don't get the worst of it, Merwell. Now let that boy go." And Dave came a step closer and clenched his fists.

"Going to help the rascal steal five dollars from me?"

"He says he knows nothing of your gold piece and he looks honest to me. Why aren't you more careful of your money?"

"He's got my gold piece and I know it!" declared Link Merwell, loudly. "If he don't pass it over, I'm going to have him arrested."

Quite a war of words followed, the loud talking attracting a crowd, including Phil and Roger and the girls. The ragged newsboy broke down completely and commenced to cry bitterly.

"This is a shame, Merwell," said the senator's son. "I think as Dave does, that the newsboy is honest. If you are so hard up, I'll give you five dollars out of my own pocket," and he produced a roll of bills.

"I don't want your money, Morr!" answered Merwell, in a rage. "I am going to make this boy give me back my gold piece."

"Say, you," said a man who had listened to the talk for several minutes. "When did you lose that five-dollar gold piece?"

"Yesterday morning," answered Link Merwell. "I bought a newspaper from this boy and after a while I found out I had given him a five-dollar piece in place of a cent."

"Did you buy any postage stamps about the same time?" went on the man.

"Why—er—yes, I did." Link Merwell gave a start. "Say, did—"

"You did," answered the man, with a sarcastic grin. "I'm the clerk at that window and I'm just going to lunch," he explained to the crowd. "You bought five two-cent stamps and threw down a nickel and what I supposed were five pennies. When I looked at them I saw one was a five-dollar gold piece. I tried to call you back, but you got out in such a hurry I couldn't locate you. If you'll come back with me I'll give you the gold piece in exchange for one cent."

"There you are, Merwell!" cried Dave. "Now you can see how you were mistaken in this boy."

Link Merwell's face was a study. He felt his humiliation keenly, and it is safe to say he would rather have lost his five dollars than have been shown up in the wrong.

"All right, I'll go back and get my gold piece," he muttered.

"I think you owe the newsboy an apology," said Phil.

"Oh, you go to thunder!" snapped Merwell, and pushed out of the crowd as fast as he could. Several followed him and saw him get his gold piece, and they passed all sorts of uncomplimentary remarks on his actions.

The girls had become interested in the ragged newsboy, and after he had picked up his newspapers, they took him to an out-of-the-way corner and questioned him. He said his name was Charley Gamp and that he was alone in the world.

"My mother died some years ago," he said. "I don't know where my father is. He left us when I was a baby."

"And do you make your living selling newspapers?" asked Laura.

Edward Stratemeyer

"Mostly, but sometimes I carry bundles and run on other errands," answered Charley Gamp.

"And where do you live?" questioned Jessie.

"Oh, I live with an old woman named Posey—that is, when I can pay for my bed. When I haven't the price I go down to the docks and find a bed among the boxes and things."

"You poor boy!" murmured Jessie, and something like tears came into her eyes. She turned to Laura. "Can't we do something for him?"

"Perhaps," answered Laura. "At any rate, we can give him some money."

The boys came over, and all had a talk with Charley Gamp, who told much about his former life, when his mother had been alive. Of his father he knew little or nothing; excepting that he had not treated his mother fairly according to the story told by some former neighbors.

"I wish we could get him some sort of regular employment and give him a chance to go to school," said Dave. "Let us ask Uncle Dunston about it. He knows quite a number of people in Chicago."

"If you want to do something for me, I'll tell you what," said Charley, eagerly. "I need a new pair of shoes." And he looked down at his foot coverings, which were full of holes.

"And I should say that you needed a new suit of clothes, too," said Laura.

"And a new cap," added Jessie. "I'll get you the cap," she went on. "A real nice one, too."

In spite of his rags and his dirty face and hands Charley Gamp had a winning way about him, and the boys and girls easily induced him to follow them to the hotel. Here they waited for the return of Dunston Porter, and then asked what might be done with the waif.

"You'll have your hands full if you want to help every waif that comes along," said Dave's uncle, with a smile. "Every big city has hundreds of them."

"Well, we can't aid every one, but we do want to aid Charley," answered Laura. And then she and the others told of what had occurred at the post-office.

"I don't know exactly how much we can do," said Dunston Porter, slowly. "I know a number of people here, it is true, but whether any of them will want to bother with this lad is a question. However, after lunch I'll look into the matter."

As the urchin was too dirty and ragged to eat in the hotel, he was given a quarter of a dollar for his dinner and told to come back in half an hour. This he did willingly, and a little later Mr. Porter, Dave, and the two girls sallied forth to see what could be done for the homeless boy.

The quest was more successful than they had anticipated. Mr. Porter knew a certain Mr. Latham, who was in the wholesale fruit business, and this gentleman agreed to give Charley Gamp a job, at two dollars a week and his board. He was to live with a man who had charge of a warehouse where fruit was unloaded, and was to be sent to night school.

This settled, the waif was fitted out with new clothing and other things, and the boys and girls and Mr. Porter made up a purse for him of twenty dollars.

"You had better put the money in a bank," said Dave. "Then you can use it as you need it,—or put more to it."

"Twenty dollars!" gasped Charley Gamp, when he saw the money. "Wow! Say, I'll be a millionaire before you know it, won't I?" And this remark caused a laugh. He promised to put the money in a savings bank, where it would draw interest, and said he would try his best to add to it from his weekly wages.

"And will you go to school regularly?" asked Mr. Porter.

"Yes, sir, I'll give you my word," replied the street boy, promptly.

"And as soon as you learn to write, you must send us letters," put in Jessie. "I shall wish to hear from you very much."

"I'll write, miss. I can write a little already—printing letters," answered Charley Gamp.

"Then here is my address," and Jessie handed over her card, and Laura did the same. Mr. Latham promised to let Mr. Porter know how the boy got along, and also promised to make some inquiries in the hope of locating the lad's father. Charley Gamp was extremely grateful for all that had been done for him, and when he parted from his new friends there were tears in his eyes.

"My mother used to tell me there was angels," he said to Jessie and Laura. "I didn't believe it much. But I do now, 'cause you're angels!" And he nodded his head earnestly, to show that he meant what he said.

"And now, ho, for the boundless West!" cried Dave, when the party was on its way to the depot. "Now for the plains and the mountains, the canyons and the rivers, the cattle and the broncos, the campfires and the cowboys, and the lasso and the rifle, the—"

"Hello, Dave is wound up!" interrupted the senator's son.

"Must have some of that ranch air in his lungs already," added Phil. "I suppose the first thing you'll want to do will be to break in a bronco, ride a couple of hundred miles, and lasso a couple of dozen buffaloes."

"Sure thing," answered Dave. "Then we'll build a roaring campfire, cook a ten-pound bear steak and eat it, shoot half a dozen Apache Indians, find a few fifteen-pound nuggets of gold, and—wake up and find the mince pie you had for supper didn't agree with you." And this unexpected ending brought forth a roar of laughter, in which even Mr. Porter joined.

"You won't find it so exciting as all that at Star Ranch," said Laura, after the others had quieted down. "But I think you'll be able to put in the time doing one thing or another."

"I reckon we'll hunt up some excitement," said the senator's son. And they did, as we shall speedily see.

CHAPTER X

OFF FOR THE BOUNDLESS WEST

"This is certainly the boundless West!"

It was Dave who spoke, and he addressed the others, who were on the rear of the observation car with him. As far as the eye could reach were the prairies, dotted here and there with hillocks and clumps of low-growing bushes. Behind were the glistening rails and the wooden ties, stretching out until lost in the distance.

A night and the larger part of the next day had been spent on the train. They had crossed the Mississippi and made several stops of more or less importance, including those at St. Paul and Minneapolis, and now they were rushing westward through North Dakota to Montana.

It was a warm, sunshiny day, and the young folk and Mr. Porter enjoyed the trip to the utmost. Dave's uncle had traveled through that section of the country several times, and he pointed out various objects of interest.

"I haven't seen any Indians yet," said Jessie, with a pout. "I thought we'd see some by this time."

"We'll see them a little further west," answered Dunston Porter. "They'll come down to the railroad stations, to sell trinkets," and his words proved true. They saw a dozen or more redmen and their squaws the following morning, at a station where they stopped for water. But the Indians were so dirty that neither Jessie nor the others wanted to trade with them, although one Indian had a set of polished horns Roger admired very much.

"Never mind, we'll get some horns at Star Ranch," said Laura. "The cowboys know how to polish them just as well as these Indians, and they'll sell their work just as cheaply, too." And this proved to be true.

They passed Livingston, which, as Dunston Porter told the young folks, was the transfer point for Yellowstone Park, and then continued on their way to Helena. Here the young folks left the train, to continue their journey on a side line running northward.

"Sorry I am not going further with you," said Dunston Porter, as he kissed his niece and shook hands warmly with the others. "I hope you get to the ranch in safety, and don't forget to send word to me at Spokane as well as to send word home."

"And you'll be sure to come to the ranch for us in about a month?" asked Laura.

"Yes, unless some special business detains me, and then I'll wire when I can come," was the reply, and then the train rolled off, Dunston Porter standing at the end, waving the boys and girls adieu.

"Now we have got to take care of ourselves," remarked the shipowner's son. "Girls, you don't feel afraid, do you?"

"Oh, we are not so very far from Star Ranch," answered Laura. "And you'll remember, I asked Mr. Endicott by telegraph to have somebody meet us. If he's at the ranch, maybe he'll come himself, and bring Belle. I know Belle will be just wild to see what sort of a brother I have found," she added, with a warm glance at Dave.

"I hope she likes me, Laura. I know I am going to like her. She's a jolly-looking girl, by her picture."

"Oh, I know she'll like you. Jessie, you had better look out!" went on Laura in a whisper, and this made Jessie turn very red. Dave heard the words and grew red, too, and commenced a lively conversation with Phil and Roger, about nothing in particular.

The train on the side line was a big contrast to the luxurious coaches they had just left. The cars were of the old-fashioned variety and but two in number, and drawn by an old mountain engine that had seen better days. Moreover, the roadbed was very uneven, and the cars rocked from side to side as they rolled between the hills towards Bramley, where the young folks were to get off. The cars were about half filled with miners and cattlemen, and a sprinkling of hunters and sight-seers, and the boys and girls overheard a good deal of talk about steers and horses, mines and new discoveries, and about the outlook for hunting and fishing.

"Why, Mr. Todd, is that you!" cried Laura, suddenly, as a cowboy was passing through the car where she sat.

"It sure is me, Miss Porter," answered the cowboy, coming to a halt with a broad grin on his weatherbeaten face. "Must be you are on your way to the ranch," he added.

"We are," answered Laura. "I am glad to see you." She held out her hand, which the cowboy took very gingerly, removing his sombrero at the same time. "This is my friend, Miss Wadsworth, and this is my brother, Dave, and his two school friends, Mr. Morr and Mr. Lawrence. This is Mr. Sidney Todd, Mr. Endicott's head man," she explained.

"Just Sid Todd, miss, that's good enough for me," said the cowboy, as the others shook hands with him, one after the other. "I ain't used to no handle, I ain't. The boss thought you might be on this train, but he wasn't sure when I left. He told me to keep an eye open for you, though. I hope you had a nice trip."

"We have had a lovely trip, Mr.—Todd," said Jessie. She could not quite bring herself to drop the mister.

"I've heard of you," said Dave to the cowboy. "My sister told me how you taught her to ride and do a lot of things. I hope you'll take me and my chums in hand, too, when we get settled at Star Ranch."

"Ride, don't you?"

"Oh, yes, but not in the fashion that cowboys can," said Dave, and then he invited Sid Todd to sit down with them, which the cowboy did. He was a man of about forty, tall and leathery. His eyes were bubbling over with good humor, but they could become very stern when the occasion demanded it. Laura had become well acquainted with him during her former visit to the ranch, and knew that the Endicotts trusted him implicitly. While he had taught her how to ride, cowgirl fashion, she had taken a number of snapshot photographs for him, to be sent to some relative in the South, and for these he had been very grateful.

"We want to do a lot of riding, and a lot of hunting and fishing, too," said the senator's son. "Do you think we'll have a chance for much sport?"

"I dunno," answered Sid Todd, dryly. "Might be the game will hear of your coming and move on to the next State," and his eyes twinkled over his little joke.

"I'd like to see some kind of a round-up," said Phil. "Will there be one while we are here?"

"Might be, Mr.—I didn't quite catch your handle."

"Phil Lawrence. Just call me Phil."

"I will if you'll call me Todd, or Sid. I can't git used to this mister business nohow. Besides, the boys would have the laugh on me, if they heard you a-mistering me all the time."

"All right, Sid it is," said Dave. "And I'm Dave."

"And I am Roger," added the senator's son.

"About that round-up," continued the cowboy. "Might see something of the sort, for Mr. Endicott is goin' to sell some cattle the end of the month, and they'll be driven off to another range. But you'll see enough of cattle anyway, before you go home, if you are going to stay a month or six weeks."

"Any fishing?" queried the shipowner's son.

"Yes, plenty of fishing, back in the mountains. One place there you can catch a barrel or two of fish in ten minutes—if you've got lines enough," and once more Sid Todd chuckled at his joke.

It was a three hours' run to Bramley, for the train stopped at many little stations and at some crossings where there were no stations at all. At one point they came to a halt where there was a large corral, and the boys and girls watched the efforts of several cowboys to lasso a bronco that was untrained. The bronco eluded the rope with apparent ease.

"Some of 'em are mighty tricky," explained Sid Todd. "I remember two years ago, we had one bronco nobody at the Star could touch. I reckon he was sure mad, for finally he bit Hank Snogger, and Hank had to treat him to a dose of lead."

"Is Hank Snogger still with Mr. Endicott?" questioned Laura.

"No, he ain't," answered Sid Todd, shortly. "He left two months ago. A good job done, too," added the cowboy.

"Who was this Hank Snogger?" asked Dave, in a low voice of

his sister, for he saw that the subject was distasteful to Todd.

"He was one of the cowboys working for Mr. Endicott," answered Laura. "He was rather a queer kind of a man."

"Bramley's just ahead," announced Sid Todd, presently. "Maybe you can catch sight of somebody you know," he added to Laura, as the train rounded the curve of a small hill.

"I see a young lady on horseback, and a man!" cried Dave's sister a few minutes later. "It's Belle, and her father! They came to meet us! Oh, I must signal to them!" And she waved her handkerchief from the car window. Soon Belle Endicott saw it, and waved her big straw hat in return.

"Welcome to the West!" she cried, merrily, as she dashed up on her pony beside the railroad tracks. "Oh, I was so afraid you wouldn't come!"

"And I was so afraid you'd miss our telegram and wouldn't meet us," returned Laura.

As soon as the train came to a stop the boys hopped down and assisted the girls to alight. Sid Todd followed, with the hand baggage, and the whole party gathered in a group, while Mr. Endicott and Belle dismounted to greet them.

"Very glad to know you," said the railroad president, with a genial smile overspreading his features. "I feel as if I knew Morr already. I have met his father and mother several times in Washington."

"Yes, so dad wrote," answered the senator's son.

"And I feel as if I knew you, and Miss Belle," said Dave. "I've heard so much about you from Laura."

"And we've heard so much about you!" cried Belle. "Oh, wasn't it simply wonderful how you found your folks! Why, it's almost like a page out of a fairy book!"

"Not quite," put in Phil. "Fairy stories aren't true, while this really happened."

"Some day Dave has got to tell me the whole story from beginning to end," said Belle. "You see, I'm going to call you Dave, and you must call me Belle."

"Well, we can't stop for stories just now," said Mr. Endicott. "It's a long ride to the ranch, and they'll be more than hungry by the time we get there. Todd, bring up the horses, and tell Jerry to dump all the baggage in the wagon. Do you all want to ride horseback, or does somebody prefer a seat in the wagon?"

"Oh, let us ride horseback, if you have animals enough!" cried Laura. "You're willing, aren't you, Jessie?"

"I—I guess so," said Jessie, rather timidly. "That is, if you don't ride too fast."

"We'll take it easy," said Belle. "And if you get tired you can wait for the wagon."

A number of sturdy-looking animals were brought up, and the entire party proceeded to mount, the boys assisting Laura and Jessie. In the meantime Sid Todd went off, to return with a ranch wagon, driven by an old man smoking a corncob pipe.

"Hello, Uncle Jerry!" cried Laura, pleasantly, and the others soon learned that the old man was known by that name and no other. He had been attached to the ranch when Mr. Endicott purchased the place, and knew no other home. He and Todd placed the baggage in the wagon, and then the cowboy swung himself into the saddle of his own steed, that had been brought to the station for him.

Just as the party was about to leave, a tall, thin, and well-dressed man dashed up, riding a coal-black steed. As he came closer Laura gave a start and motioned for Dave to come closer.

"Who is it?" asked Dave, in a low voice.

"That is Mr. Merwell," answered his sister.

CHAPTER XI

THE ARRIVAL AT STAR RANCH

Mr. Felix Merwell bowed stiffly to Mr. Endicott, and, on seeing Laura, raised his hat slightly. Both of the others bowed in return. Then the eyes of the newcomer swept the vicinity of the little railroad station.

"See anything of my son, Link?" he asked, of Sid Todd.

"No, sir," was the short reply. It was quite evident that the cowboy and the ranch owner were not on very friendly terms.

"Humph! I thought sure he'd be on this train," muttered Mr. Merwell, to no one in particular. He looked at the boys. "You came in on the train that just left, I suppose," he said.

"We did," answered Dave.

"See anything of a boy about your own age in Helena, at the depot? He was coming on the eastern train."

"Your son wasn't on the train," answered Dave.

"Ah! you know him?"

"Yes."

"Who are you, may I ask? I do not remember seeing

you before."

"I am Dave Porter. Link and I went to Oak Hall together."

"Ah, I see!" Mr. Merwell drew a long breath and nodded his head knowingly. "Dave Porter, you said. And who are these young men?"

"My school chums, Roger Morr and Phil Lawrence."

"Indeed! Then you are the young men who caused my son so much trouble—caused him to be sent away, in fact," continued Mr. Merwell, and he glared hatefully at the three lads.

"It was Link's own fault that he was sent away," answered the senator's son. "If he had behaved himself he would have had no trouble."

"Oh, of course, it is natural that you should shield yourselves. But I know my son, and I know he is not the person he has been made out to be by Doctor Clay and others. It was an outrage to allow the other boys at the school to get him into trouble as they did, and I have written to Doctor Clay to that effect."

"Your son was entirely to blame," said Phil, bound to stand up for himself.

"He can be thankful that he was let off so easily," added Dave. "If it hadn't been for the honor of Oak Hall, there might have been a public exposure."

"Bah! nonsense! But it is useless to continue this discussion here, in the presence of these young ladies. Perhaps I'll see you again about the matter—after I have interviewed my son personally."

"Mr. Merwell, these young gentleman are my guests," put in Mr. Endicott, bluntly. "While they are stopping at my ranch I trust they will not be annoyed by any one."

"Mr. Endicott, I shall respect your wishes so far as I can," returned Felix Merwell, with great stiffness. "But if these young men have done my son an injustice, they will have to suffer for it. I bid you good-day." And having thus delivered himself, the man wheeled around his coal-black steed and was off in a cloud of dust down the road.

"Oh, Dave, what do you think he'll do?" asked Jessie, in alarm.

"I don't know," was Dave's reply. "Of course, he is bound to stick up for Link."

"I never liked him very much, and now I despise him," said Laura.

"One can readily see where Link gets his temper from," was Phil's comment. "He is nothing but a chip of the old block."

"I am sorry that Mr. Merwell is my neighbor," came from Mr. Endicott. "But it can't be helped, so we'll have to make the best of it. My advice is, while you are out here, keep off his lands, and if he annoys you in any way, let me know."

"We'll have to learn what his lands are," said the senator's son.

"Todd and the others can readily tell you about that, and about Merwell's cattle, too. But come, we have wasted too much time already. You'll all be wanting supper long before we reach the ranch."

Old Jerry had gone ahead with the wagon, and now the others followed along the road taken by the turnout and by Mr. Merwell. It was a winding trail, leading up and down over the hills and through a dense patch of timber. Two miles from the station they had to cross a fair-sized stream by way of a bridge that was far from firm.

"We've got to have a new bridge here some day," said Mr. Endicott. "I am willing to bear my share of the expense, but Merwell won't put up a cent. He doesn't go in for improvements."

"He seems to like good horseflesh," remarked Phil.

"That was one of his best mounts. His horses aren't half as good as those we have; eh, Todd?"

"No better bosses in these parts than those at the Star," answered the cowboy.

"I have been giving our horses my especial care for three years," explained the railroad president. "It has become a hobby with me, and some day I may turn the ranch into something of a stock farm for raising certain breeds of horses and ponies. While you are here you'll not suffer for the want of a mount."

"I'd like to see you break in some of the horses," said Roger.

"Well, you'll have the chance."

"Maybe you'd like to break in a bronco yourself," suggested Belle, with a twinkle in her eye.

"And get sent skyhigh!" returned the senator's son. "No, thank you, not until I've learned the business."

"A bronco is all right if you understand him," remarked Sid Todd. "But if you don't, you'd better monkey with the business end of a gun,—it's just as healthy."

The woods left behind, they commenced to ascend a long hill. Far off to the westward loomed the mountains, covered with pines and bordered below with cottonwoods.

"There is where you'll get your hunting when you want it," said Mr. Endicott. "How is it, can you shoot?"

"We can," answered Phil, and then told of some of their experiences in the South Sea islands. Then Roger told of the adventures which Dave and he had in Norway, and Dave ended by telling of the target practice with the swinging board.

"Well, I'll tell you right now a big bear out in them mountains ain't no swingin' board," said Sid Todd. "He's a whole lumber yard, when he's cornered." And at this remark there was a general laugh.

It was getting dark when they came in sight of Star Ranch. They made out a long, low building on the southern slope of a small hill. It was built in modern bungalow fashion, having been erected by Mr. Endicott after the original log dwelling had been destroyed by fire. It was divided into a sitting-room fifteen feet by twenty-five, an office, a good-sized dining-hall, a kitchen, and eight bedrooms, and a bath. Water was pumped from a brook at the foot of the hill, and the rooms were lighted by a new system of gasoline gas. The ranch home was comfortably furnished, and in the sitting-room were a bookcase filled with good reading, and a new player piano, with a combination cabinet of sheet music and music rolls.

"I play by hand," said Belle, when the boys noticed the player piano, "but papa plays with his feet."

"That's the kind of playing I do, too," answered Phil, with a grin.

"But you sing, don't you?" asked the young hostess of the ranch.

"Oh, yes, we all sing."

"Belle is a beautiful player," said Laura. "Wait till you hear her play some operatic selections."

Supper was in readiness, having been ordered in advance by Mrs. Endicott, a sweet woman who looked like Laura, and as soon as the girls and boys had had a chance to brush up and wash, all sat down to partake of the good things provided. Jessie was much astonished by the things spread before her.

"Why, I thought we were going to live in regular camping style!" she declared. "This is as good as what we had at the hotel in Chicago, if not better."

"The Wild West of to-day is not the Wild West of years ago," explained Mrs. Endicott. "People from the East have a wrong impression of many things. Of course some things are still crude, but others are as up-to-date as any one could wish."

"What I like best of all is the general open-heartedness of the people you meet," declared Dave. "They are not quite so frozen-up as in some places in the East."

"That is true, and it is readily explained," answered the ranch owner. "In the pioneer days everybody had to depend upon everybody else, and consequently all were more or less sociable. The feeling has not yet worn off. But I am afraid it will wear off, as we become more and more what is called civilized," added Mr. Endicott, with something of a sigh.

Everybody was hungry, and all did full justice to the repast. As they ate, the boys and girls asked many questions concerning the ranch and the neighborhood generally, and Mr. and Mrs. Endicott and Belle were kept busy answering first one and then another. The railroad president told how he had come to purchase the place—doing it for the sake of his health—and mentioned the many improvements he had made.

"We used to simply corral the horses and cattle," said he. "But now I have a fine stable for the horses, and numerous sheds for the cattle. We have also big barns for hay and grain, and a hen-house with a run fifty feet by two hundred."

"The chickens are my pets," said Belle. "I have some of the cutest bantams you ever saw."

"I'll help you feed them," said Jessie. At Crumville she had always taken an interest in the chickens.

The trunks and dress-suit cases had been brought in by old Jerry and one of the Chinese servants, and placed in the proper rooms, and after supper the boys and girls spent an hour in getting settled. Laura and Jessie had a nice room that connected with one occupied by Belle, and Dave, Phil, and Roger were assigned to two rooms directly opposite.

"You boys can divide up the rooms to suit yourselves," said Mrs. Endicott.

"Thank you, we will," they answered, and later arranged that Dave was to have one apartment and Roger the other, and Phil was to sleep one week with one chum and the next with the other.

"Say, but this suits me down to the ground!" cried the senator's son, after the boys had said good-night to the others. "It's a complete surprise. Like Jessie, I had an idea we'd have to rough it."

"I knew about what to expect, for Laura told me," answered Dave, with a smile. "I didn't say too much because I wanted you to be surprised. But it's better even than I anticipated. If we don't have the outing of our lives here, it will be our own fault."

"The Endicotts are certainly fine folks," said the shipowner's son, as he sat on the edge of a bed to unlace his shoes. "And Belle is—well, as nice as they make 'em."

"Hello, Phil must be smitten!" cried Roger. "Well, I don't blame you, old man."

"Who said I was smitten?" returned Phil, his face growing red. "I said she was a dandy girl, that's all."

"And she is," said Dave. "I don't wonder Laura likes her."

"We ought to be able to make up some fine parties," continued Phil, as he dropped a shoe on the floor. "Dave can take out Jessie, and you can take out Laura, and I'll—"

"Take out Miss Belle," finished the senator's son. He caught Phil by the foot. "Say, you're smitten all right. Come on, Dave, let us wake him out of his dream!" And he commenced to pull on the foot.

"Hi! you let up!" cried the shipowner's son, clutching at the bed to keep himself from falling to the floor. "I haven't said half as much about Belle as you've said about Laura, so there!"

"Never said anything about Laura!" answered Roger, but he, too, turned red. Dave commenced to laugh heartily, and Phil wrenched himself free and stood up.

"What's sauce for the goose is sauce for the gander," cried Dave. "Better both quit your knocking and go to bed. I suppose the girls are tired out and want to go to sleep."

"Sounds like it, doesn't it," murmured Roger, as a shriek of laughter came from across the hallway.

"Maybe they are knocking each other the same way," suggested Phil.

"Never!" cried Dave. "Girls aren't built that way."

But Dave was mistaken.

A little later quietness reigned, and one after another the newcomers to Star Ranch dropped asleep.

Edward Stratemeyer

CHAPTER XII

A RACE ON HORSEBACK

"What a beautiful spot!"

It was Dave who uttered the words, as he stood out in front of the ranch house on the following morning. He had gotten up early, and Laura and Belle had joined him, leaving the others still at rest.

Dave spoke with feeling, for the grand and sublime things in Nature had always appealed to him. He was gazing toward the east, where the rising sun was flooding the plains with a golden hue. Beyond the cottonwoods he caught a glimpse of the winding river. Then, when he turned, he saw the foothills and the mountains in the west, with their great bowlders and cliffs and their sturdy growths of pine.

"Aren't you glad you came, Dave?" said his sister, as she placed an affectionate hand on his shoulder.

"Indeed I am, Laura," he replied. "Why, it looks to me as if I was going to have the outing of my life! In fact, all of us ought to have the best time ever!"

"Does it put you in mind of your trip to Norway?" questioned Belle.

"Hardly. That was taken during cold weather, and everything was covered with snow and ice. Besides, the scenery was quite different." Dave paused to sweep the horizon. "In what direction is the Merwell ranch?" he asked.

"Over yonder," answered Belle, pointing up the river. "The little brook flowing down between those rough rocks marks the boundary line."

"And whose cattle are those on yonder hills?"

"I am not sure, but I think they belong to papa. When you ask about cattle you must go to Sid Todd. He knows every animal for miles around."

"I suppose your cattle are all branded?"

"Oh, yes, with a star and the letter E on either side of it. That's why this is called Star Ranch."

"What is the Merwell brand?" asked Laura.

"A triple cross."

Breakfast was soon announced, and all the girls and boys assembled in the dining-hall. While they ate the meal, Mr. Endicott told the newcomers much about his ranch, and also about the people working for him.

"I am sorry to hear that you have had trouble with Mr. Merwell's son," said the railroad president. "I am afraid it will make matters worse out here—and they are bad enough as it is."

"But I am sure Dave and his chums are not to blame, Mr. Endicott," said Laura, hastily.

"Oh, I am sure of that myself—for I know something of Link Merwell and his headstrong temper,—a temper he gets largely from his father. If it were not for that temper, I think Mr.

Merwell and myself might be on better terms."

"We have had trouble over one of the hired men, Hank Snogger," explained Belle. "Snogger used to work for us, but Mr. Merwell hired him away."

"That wasn't a very nice thing to do," was Roger's comment.

"If it had been done openly it would not have been so bad," said Mr. Endicott. "But it was done secretly, and Snogger was gone almost before I knew it. He was a valuable man and I felt his loss keenly."

"I suppose Mr. Merwell offered him more wages," said Phil.

"Probably, although I paid Snogger a good salary. I don't know what game Merwell played to get the fellow, but he got him."

"It's exactly like some of Link's underhanded work at Oak Hall," was Roger's comment. "Father and son must be very much alike."

"While you are here I would advise you to steer clear of the Merwells," was Mr. Endicott's advice. "I'd not even go on their land if you can help it. There are plenty of other places to go to."

"I'll not go near his ranch, if I know it," answered Dave.

"It is queer that Link did not come on the train with you, if his father was expecting him."

"Oh, most likely he stopped off somewhere to have a good time," answered the senator's son. "A fellow like Link would be apt to find life slow on a ranch."

After breakfast Mr. Endicott and Belle took the boys and girls around the ranch buildings, which were quite numerous. The girls were interested in some fancy chickens and pigeons Belle owned, and the boys grew enthusiastic over the horses.

"I never saw better animals!" cried Dave, his eyes resting on a black horse that was truly a beauty. "What's his name?" he asked.

"Hero," answered Mr. Endicott. "He can go, let me tell you. You can try him this afternoon, if you wish."

"Thank you, perhaps I will."

"And if you like him, you can use Hero during your stay here," went on the railroad president, and then he pointed out various horses that the others might use.

"No busting broncos here, I suppose," said Phil, with a grin.

"No. If you want to try a bronco, you'll have to see Todd. But I advise you to be careful. Some day I'll have Todd give you an exhibition of bronco busting, as it is called."

During their tour of the place they met several cowboys and other helpers, and soon became well acquainted. In the past, visitors to Star Ranch had been numerous, consequently the most of the men were not as shy as they might otherwise have been. They gladly answered all the questions the boys and girls put to them, and offered to do all sorts of things to render the visit of the newcomers pleasant.

After lunch the girls felt like resting, for it was rather warm, but all the boys were anxious to get into the saddle. They had heard that Sid Todd was going to a distant part of the range, to see about two steers that had fallen into a ravine, and asked to be taken along.

"All right, my boys," said the cowboy. "Come ahead. But you'll have to do quite a bit of riding to get there and back by nightfall."

"Well, we may as well get used to it," answered Phil. "I expect to about live in the saddle while I am here."

Todd had several things to attend to before starting, so they did not leave the stables until nearly three o'clock. Dave was mounted on the steed he had so admired, and the others had equally good horses.

"Shall we take our guns?" asked Roger.

"What for?" asked the cowboy.

"Oh, I thought we might get the chance to shoot something."

"We'll not have much time to look for game," answered Sid Todd. "However, if you want to take your shootin' irons, there ain't no objections." So each of the lads provided himself with a shotgun. Todd carried a pistol, of the "hoss" variety and nearly two feet long, the same being deposited in the holster of his saddle.

The course was to the westward, to the foothills of the distant mountains. Here, the cowboy explained, was a treacherous ravine, the sides overgrown with a tangle of low bushes. The cattle loved to get in the bushes, finding something there particularly appetizing to eat, and often the rocks and dirt would give way and a steer would go down in the hollow and be unable to get out.

"They don't seem to know how to climb the rocks," said Sid Todd. "And you've got to fairly drive 'em the right way, or they'd stay in the hollow till they died."

Dave felt like "letting himself loose," as he expressed it, and with a level stretch of several miles before them, he called on Phil and Roger for a race.

"Done!" cried the shipowner's son. "But I know you'll beat," he added. "You've had more practice on horseback than I have had."

"Take care and keep to the trail!" sung out Sid Todd. He had no desire to join in the sport, for horseback riding was no novelty to him.

Over the soft ground thundered the three horses, the boys at the start keeping in a bunch. But gradually they spread out and then Roger forged ahead.

"Here is where I win!" sang out the senator's son.

"Not much!" answered Phil. "Just wait till my horse gets his muscles limbered up a bit!" And then he urged his animal to a better gait, and slowly but surely crawled up closer to Roger.

Dave said but little, for he was paying all his attention to Hero. He had studied horses from childhood, and he thought he saw in the steed he rode better staying qualities than in either of the other animals. He kept on directly behind his chums, but made no effort for the first half mile to pass them.

"How far do we race?" cried the senator's son, presently.

"To the patch of woods," answered Dave, indicating a growth about a mile distant.

"All right—and—good-by to you!" returned Roger, merrily.

"Dave, you aren't in it a little bit!" added Phil. And he sped after the senator's son, leaving Dave a full fifty yards in the rear.

Dave saw that Hero was gradually warming up to his task. He clucked softly, and the little black horse pricked up his ears and increased his gait. Then Dave clucked again—he had heard Todd do this—and Hero went a little faster.

On went the three boys, the fresh air of the plains and the

Edward Stratemeyer

mountains filling their lungs and causing their eyes to snap with pure delight. At that moment each of them felt as if he hadn't a care in the world.

Phil and Roger were now neck-and-neck, with not quite half a mile of the race still to cover. Sixty yards behind was Dave. Still further to the rear was Sid Todd, now urging his horse forward, that he might see the finish of the contest.

"Now, then, my little beauty, go!" cried Dave to his horse, and he clucked several times to Hero, and dug his heels into the steed's ribs.

He had not miscalculated, and Hero responded instantly. Up he went into the air, and when he came down his ears were laid far back, and forward he shot like an arrow from a bow. Dave kept him to it, and gradually he ranged up between the others.

"Hi, get back there!" yelled Roger, who was now slightly in advance. "You can beat Phil, but you can't beat me!"

"Not much! He's not going to beat me!" put in the shipowner's son, and he urged his horse to do better. But this was impossible, and, inch by inch, Dave overtook him, and went to the front.

It now seemed to be a race between Hero and the brown horse that the senator's son rode. Roger's mount was still in fine condition, but it must be confessed that the senator's son did not know exactly how to race him to the best advantage. He sawed a little on the reins, thus worrying the animal, and causing him to lose his gait. Then, with a bound, Dave came up, and the pair were neck-and-neck for the finish.

"Go! go!" yelled Phil. "May the best horse win!"

"Whoopee!" came unexpectedly from Sid Todd, and, grabbing his pistol from the holster, he sent three shots into the air, just to add to the excitement.

As the pistol went off, both horses gave an extra bound forward. The two young riders were almost unseated, but each quickly recovered. Then they bent low over their steeds' necks and went forward for the finish.

It was a thrilling moment, Dave and Roger side by side, Phil at their heels, and Sid Todd further back, firing another shot or two, "just for fun," in true cowboy fashion.

But Roger had urged his horse to the limit and could do no better. As Dave clucked again, Hero shot ahead, a foot, a yard, and soon several yards. Then Phil came up abreast of the senator's son, and thus they kept until the edge of the woods was gained.

"Dave wins!" cried Sid Todd. "An' a good race, boys,—a good race all around."

"Yes, Dave wins!" answered Phil. "My, but your horse did go it at the finish!" he added, admiringly.

"A fine animal," said Roger. "But mine is fine, too, even if he didn't come in first," he added, loyally.

"You all rode well—better nor I expected," was Sid Todd's comment. "It was a good race. I wish the others on the ranch had seen it,—they wouldn't call you tenderfeet no more!"

CHAPTER XIII

THE CRAZY STEER

In the shade of the woods the boys rested their steeds for a few minutes, and as they did this the cowboy told them of some of the races he had seen in the past on Star Ranch.

"One of the greatest races was between one o' the cowboys and an Indian named Crowfoot Joe," said the cowboy. "The Indian was sure he was going to win, but he lost by a neck. That race took place two years ago, but the boys in these parts ain't done tellin' about it yet. We had a full holiday the time it come off."

"I think your horse is just as good as mine," said Dave to Roger. "But I fancy you pressed him a little too hard at the start."

"He is just as good, an' so is the hoss Phil is ridin'," came from Sid Todd. "It was the ridin' did it. Dave managed his mount just right." And this open praise made the youth from Crumville blush.

"Just wait till Jessie hears how he won," said the shipowner's son. "She'll weave a laurel crown for his brow and—"

"Don't you say a word about it!" cried Dave, and blushed more than ever. "I didn't win by so very much, anyway."

Forward the party went, through the woods, and then in the direction of the foothills beyond. The race had not hurt the horses in the least, for all of them were tough and used to hard usage. They were following a well-defined trail, but presently branched off to the southward and commenced to climb the first of the hills.

"That hollow is about quarter of a mile from here," explained the cowboy. "Be careful now, or your horse will get into a hole, an' maybe break a leg." And then they went forward with added caution, into the midst of a growth of low bushes, dotted here and there with sagebrush.

Presently the cowboy uttered a long, loud whistle and this was answered by somebody near the edge of the ravine. Then another ranch hand named Tom Yates showed himself. He was on foot, but his horse was tethered not far away.

"Well, where are they?" asked Todd, of the other cowboy.

"Where are they?" growled Tom Yates. "Where they always are when they go over, hang 'em! Say, we're going to have a fierce job this time," he added.

"Why?" asked Todd.

"Because that big steer—the spotted one—went over with two of the others. He got hurt a few days ago in the woods, and he's as ugly as sin because of it."

"Well, we'll have to drive 'em up, same as we did before," answered Sid Todd, briefly.

"I don't think you'll drive that steer," answered Tom Yates. "Blinky and I tried it, and we couldn't do a thing with him. Blinky wouldn't stay here. He thinks the steer is crazy."

"Got a rope?"

"Sure," was the answer, and the cowboy who had been working to get the cattle out of the ravine, swung a strong lasso into view. "But you ain't goin' to use that on that steer," he continued. "Leas'wise, not if you want to live to tell it."

"We'll see," answered Sid Todd, briefly, as he dismounted and took the lasso.

"Can we help?" asked Dave.

"Sure you can," answered the cowboy who had accompanied the boys. "Just you keep out of the way, an' that will be all the help we need."

"But perhaps we could do something," grumbled Roger. "I want to get into a regular round-up of cattle some day."

"This ain't no round-up, my boy. If you go down into the hollow those cattle will be wuss frightened nor ever. You just stay up here and watch things. I'm going to get 'em out—or know the reason why," finished Sid Todd, and he walked away with Tom Yates, and presently the pair were joined by a third hand, the fellow who had said he thought one of the steers was crazy.

With nothing else to do, the three boys dismounted, tethered their steeds, and walked slowly and cautiously to the edge of the ravine. The ground was very uneven, and treacherous holes were numerous.

"You would think there would be a lot of game around here," was Dave's comment. "But so far I haven't seen a thing."

"I think the cattle and the cowboys have scared the animals away," answered Roger. "For hunting we'll have to go where it is even wilder than this—Todd said so."

"My, but this air is the finest ever!" cried Phil. "I declare, it makes me feel young!"

"As if he were old!" protested the senator's son. "But the air is great!" he added.

"I know what it does to me," declared Dave. "Makes me mighty hungry."

"Same here," answered the shipowner's son. "I think I could eat about six square meals a day. When we go out hunting, for a full day or more, we mustn't forget to take plenty of food along."

"Oh, we'll eat what we shoot, Phil," said Dave, with a wink at Roger. "They always do that out West, you know."

"Huh! And if we don't shoot we can starve, eh? Not much! I'm going to take plenty of good things along when I go out."

"I wonder if we'll see much of Link Merwell," said Roger, after a pause.

"I don't want to see him," answered Dave.

"But he'll see you, Dave. Didn't he say he'd square accounts out here? He'll keep his word—when it comes to doing anything mean and dirty."

"Roger is right," said Phil. "I shouldn't want to alarm the girls, or Mr. and Mrs. Endicott, but I'd surely keep my eyes open for Link Merwell. He'll try some kind of a game—it's his nature."

With caution the boys approached the edge of the ravine and looked over. They saw a spot where the dirt, rocks, and bushes had torn loose and slid down to the bottom of the hollow, carrying with the mass three of Mr. Endicott's herd of cattle. Two of the herd had been driven up to safety by the cowboys, but the third—the vicious steer—was still below, unable to help himself, and showing fight whenever approached by the ranch hands.

"I see him!" announced Phil, pointing with his hand to some rocks below. "He looks peaceful enough."

"So does a bomb—until it goes off," answered Dave. "The cowboys wouldn't be afraid of him unless he was a bad one. Maybe he is really crazy. I've heard of a crazy horse."

"Say, that puts me in mind of a story Shadow Hamilton told," came from the senator's son. "A boy in school was a regular blockhead, and one day the teacher asked him what made him so foolish. 'I dunno,' he answered, 'excepting that my mother makes me sleep under a crazy quilt.'"

"Say, that's like Shadow!" cried Phil, after a laugh all around. "Wish he was here—what stories he would tell!"

For some little time the boys could not see the men, who were hidden by the rocks and brushwood. But presently they caught sight of Sid Todd. He was flourishing a stick at the steer. The animal paid no attention at first, but presently commenced to shake his head from side to side.

"Doesn't like it," was Roger's comment.

"He seems to be saying 'No' quite forcibly," added Dave.

"Now Todd is after him," cried the shipowner's son a minute later. "See, the steer is on the move at last."

"Yes, but he is going after Todd!" answered Roger.

Such was the fact, and presently man and beast disappeared behind some brushwood. Then, when they emerged again, it was seen that the cowboy had lassoed the animal by one of the forelegs. He was mounting the rocks, and the steer was limping behind, trying vainly to shake himself free. He did not seem to know enough to hold back altogether.

"Well, I think that rather dangerous!" declared Phil.

"Supposing the steer should run for him?"

"I guess the cowboy knows what he is doing," answered Dave. "If he is pursued, he can easily scramble up on some of the steep rocks and get out of the way."

For fully ten minutes they watched the scene below them with interest. At one time the cowboy would appear to have the best of the situation, then it looked as if the steer would have his own way. But gradually man and beast worked up toward the top of the ravine.

"He'll worry the steer along, if he doesn't get too tired," said Dave. "But it must be a fearful strain on him."

The strain was heavier than the boys anticipated and several times Sid Todd was on the point of giving up the struggle. Perhaps, had he been alone, he might have done so. But, with the others looking on, he felt that his reputation was at stake, and so he worried along, until he suddenly slipped on some rocks and fell flat.

As he went down, the steer appeared to realize the man's helplessness, and with a weird snort he rushed forward, the lasso becoming tangled up on the front leg as he advanced.

"Look out, Sid!" yelled Yates. "He's goin' to hook yer!"

Todd had been a little stunned by his fall, and a bit of brush-wood hid the animal from his view. But at the cry of alarm from the other ranch hand he realized his peril and rolled over, between two tall rocks.

On came the steer and struck one of the rocks a blow that resounded loudly through the ravine. Then the beast gave a leap, directly over Todd's body, and landed on the rocks beyond.

"Is he hurt?" asked Roger, anxiously.

"I don't know, but I don't think so," answered Dave.

"See, the steer is coming right up the side of the ravine!" cried Phil. "He is dragging the lasso after him."

"Yes, and he is coming this way!" put in the senator's son. "Perhaps we had better get out of the way!" he added, in alarm.

"Oh, I don't think he'll tackle us," answered Phil.

"There is no telling what he will do," said Dave. "He is coming to the top, that is sure. Maybe we had better get into the saddle. We'll be safer on horseback."

The horses of the three boys were tethered some distance away, and as mentioned before, the lads had to move slowly, for fear of stepping into some hole. As they advanced they heard loud cries coming up from the bottom of the ravine.

"What can be wrong down there now?" questioned the shipowner's son.

"I don't know," returned Roger. "Perhaps they are shouting to warn us."

"That is just what they are doing!" added Dave, quickly. "Listen!"

"Look out, up there!" came from the ravine. "Look out! The steer is coming!"

The boys quickened their pace, but hardly had they covered half the distance to where the horses were tied when Roger suddenly slipped and went down.

"Hurry up!" called out Phil, who was near.

"Oh!" moaned the senator's son, and his face took on a look

of pain.

"What's wrong?" asked Dave, coming up.

"My foot! It got twisted, and now it is fast in the hole!" answered Roger. "Gracious! how it hurts!" he went on, making a wry face.

"Come! come!" urged Dave. "That steer is coming! There he is now!" And he pointed to the lower end of the ravine, where the animal had just bobbed up among the bushes, shaking his head from side to side in a queer, uncanny way.

Roger tried to pull his foot from between the rocks, but was unable to do so. Phil had run on, thinking his chums would follow. Dave stopped short.

"Can't you make it, Roger?" he asked, anxiously, and with another glance in the direction of the steer. The animal was now in full view.

"I—I—don't seem to be—be able to!" panted the senator's son. "Oh, if only that steer doesn't come this way!" he went on, in fresh alarm.

"He is coming this way!" exclaimed Dave. "Oh, Roger, let me help you!" And now he bent over and tried with might and main to get his chum's foot free. As he did this the steer came forward slowly. Then the animal gave an unexpected snort of rage and charged full tilt at the helpless youth.

CHAPTER XIV

A FACE PUZZLES DAVE

It was a time of extreme peril for Roger, and no one realized it more fully than did Dave. The angry steer was still some distance away, but coming forward at his best speed. One prod from those horns and the senator's son would be killed or badly hurt.

As said before, Phil had gone on, thinking his chums would follow. He was already at the side of his horse, and speedily untied the animal, and vaulted into the saddle.

"Why, what's up?" he cried, in dismay, as he turned, to behold Roger in the hole and Dave beside him.

"Roger's foot is fast!" answered Dave. "Oh, Phil, see if you can't scare the steer off!"

"I'll do what I can," came from the shipowner's son, and rather timidly, it must be confessed, he advanced on the animal in question. He gave a loud shout and swung his arm, and the steer looked toward him and came to a halt.

"You've got your gun—if he tries to horn Roger, shoot him," went on Dave.

"I will," answered Phil, and riding still closer he swung his firearm around for action.

Dave made a hasty examination and saw that Roger's foot was caught by the toe and the heel, and would have to be turned in a side-way fashion to be loosened. He caught his chum under the arms and turned him partly over.

"Now try it," he said quickly, at the same time turning once more to look at the steer. The beast had finished his inspection of Phil and was coming forward as before, with head and horns almost sweeping the ground. Behind him trailed the long lasso, which was still fast to one of his forelegs.

"Phil! Phil!" cried Dave, suddenly. "I have it! Catch the lasso if you can and hold him back!"

"I will—if I can," was the ready response. And making a semicircle the shipowner's son came up behind the steer, leaped to the ground, caught hold of the lasso, and sprang back into the saddle, almost as quick as it takes to tell it. Then he made the rope fast to his pommel and turned his horse back.

The steer was but two yards away from Roger and Dave when the rope on his foreleg suddenly tightened, and he found himself brought to a halt. He gave a wild snort, and, just as Roger found himself at liberty, he turned and gazed angrily at Phil and his steed. Then he charged in that direction.

"Ride for it, Phil!" called Dave, but this warning was unnecessary, for the shipowner's son was already galloping across the field as rapidly as the nature of the ground permitted. The horse easily kept the lasso taut, thus worrying the steer not a little.

By Dave's aid Roger managed to hobble to where the other horses were tethered, and soon both boys were in the saddle and riding after Phil and the steer.

"I guess the steer is getting winded," said Dave, coming closer. "He doesn't seem to have as much fight in him as he did."

Edward Stratemeyer

Around and around, in a broad circle, went Phil and his horse and the steer. But the steps of the latter were slower and slower, and presently the beast dropped into a walk and then refused to take another step. Phil came to a halt also, but kept the lasso tight. Then the steer lay down on his side.

"I guess he is conquered," was Roger's comment.

The three boys kept at a safe distance and waited for the appearance of Sid Todd and the other cowboys. Presently Todd came over the rim of the ravine and looked around anxiously.

"Anybody hurt?" he questioned, as he ran forward.

"Roger got his ankle twisted, running away from the steer," answered Dave.

"What did the critter do?" went on the cowboy, and Phil and the others told their story, to which Sid Todd listened with interest. The other cowboys also came up, to look the fallen steer over.

"He sure is a crazy one," said Yates. "If I was the boss, I'd shoot him."

"I'll report about him as soon as I get back," answered Todd. "Say, you had a nerve to take hold of this lasso," he went on to Phil.

"Dave told me to do it," was the answer of the shipowner's son. "It was easy enough—when I was on horseback. I shouldn't have done it if I had been on foot."

"Not much—unless you're a staving good runner," said Yates, with a grin.

The steer was too exhausted to make further resistance just then, and the cowboys had but little trouble in taking the lasso from his foreleg.

"He'll be all right after a bit," said Todd, in answer to a question from Dave. "But I think myself he isn't just O. K. in his head, and the next time we want some fresh meat we might as well kill him off and be done with it."

The cowboy insisted upon looking at Roger's ankle. The member was somewhat swollen, but the senator's son said it would not bother him to ride home. In a little while they were off in a bunch. When quite a distance from the ravine they gazed back and saw that the steer had gotten up and was grazing as if nothing out of the ordinary had happened.

"Well, we have put in a rather strenuous day for a starter," remarked Dave, when they came in sight of the ranch home. "If this keeps up—"

"But it won't," interrupted Phil. "I reckon some days will be dull enough."

The girls were awaiting their return, and they listened with keen attention to what the boys had to tell.

"You must bathe your ankle with liniment," cried Belle. "I'll get some for you," and soon she presented Roger with the stuff. He did as directed, and soon the swollen member felt far more comfortable. During the evening the senator's son took it easy on the wide veranda and in the sitting-room.

"I wish I had seen the race!" cried Jessie, smiling at Dave. "Some day you'll have to have another and let us girls look on."

"What's the matter with you girls having a race?" queried Dave. "That would be dead loads of fun—for us boys."

"Belle would be sure to win—she can ride like the wind," answered Laura.

As soon as it grew dark that evening the girls and boys went indoors, and played and sang. Belle showed her skill on the piano, and Dave and Phil tried the mechanical arrangement of the instrument, with perforated music rolls. Almost before they realized it, it was time to go to bed.

The next morning Roger still limped a little, and it was agreed to take it easy. All wanted to write letters, and the entire day was spent in doing little else.

"How will the letters be posted?" asked Dave.

"Todd will take them over to the railroad station to-morrow," answered Mrs. Endicott.

Shortly after dinner the next day, the cowboy announced that he was ready to take the mail to the station. Phil and Roger had wandered off to the barns, to look at some calves.

"If you don't mind, I'll go with you to the station," said Dave to the cowboy. "The ride would just suit me."

"Glad to have you along," answered Sid Todd. He had taken a strong fancy to the boys and to Dave in particular.

They were soon on their way, Todd carrying the mail in a bag slung over his horse's neck. Man and boy were in the best of spirits, and both made rapid time over the dusty roads.

"Maybe you'll meet a friend of yours at the station when the train comes in," said Todd.

"A friend? Who?" asked Dave.

"That Merwell boy. Yates heard he was coming to-day. One of the cowboys from Merwell's ranch said so."

"I don't know that I care to meet him," answered Dave. "He is no friend of mine."

"That boy ought to have his hide tanned good and proper," growled the cowboy. "He's been a sore spot here for years."

"Have you had trouble with him?"

"Yes, and so has everybody else on this ranch, and on his own ranch, too, for the matter of that. Not that he did anything very bad," continued Todd. "But it's jest his mean, measly ways. He don't know how to treat a hand civilly."

"Isn't his father the same way?"

"Sometimes, but not always. The old man knows that the boys won't stand for too much of that thing."

"Who is at their ranch besides Mr. Merwell?"

"Oh, the regular hands, that's all."

"No young folks?"

"No."

"I should think it would be lonely for Link."

"Maybe it is. But that ain't no reason why he should act so mean," added Sid Todd.

"I should think he'd want to invite some of his friends to visit him."

"Maybe Mr. Merwell don't want it. He's putty close, you must remember, and it costs money to entertain."

"Well, I pity Link if he has got to stay there alone."

"He don't stay all the time. He rides to town, and smokes and gambles, and gets into all sorts of trouble, and then he gets scared to death for fear the old man will find it out," concluded Sid Todd.

They were soon at the station, and there found they would have to wait half an hour for the train to come in. Several cowboys were present and also a gentleman with a white, flowing beard.

"That is Mr. Hooper," said Sid Todd. "He owns a ranch up the river—the Bar X. He's a fine man." And a few minutes later he introduced Dave to the ranch owner.

"Glad to know you," said Mr. Hooper. "I heard that my friend, Endicott, had a lot of boys and girls at his place. Tell Belle she must bring all of you over to my place some day."

"Thank you, I will," answered Dave.

"We haven't any boys and girls there, but I reckon we can give you a good time," went on Mr. Hooper.

Among the cowboys at the station, Dave noticed one tall and particularly powerful fellow. His face looked somewhat familiar, and the Crumville youth wondered if he had met the man before.

"That is Hank Snogger, the fellow who left our place to work for Mr. Merwell," said Sid Todd, in a low voice.

"His face looks familiar to me, but I can't place him," returned Dave. "Did he come from the East?"

"I think he did, years ago. Think you know him?"

"It seems to me I've met him before—or met somebody that looked like him," answered Dave, slowly. He was trying in vain to place those features.

"Don't you remember the name?"

"No."

"We ain't on very good terms any more, otherwise I'd give you a knock-down to him," went on the cowboy.

"I don't know that I care for an introduction," answered Dave. "He doesn't look like a person I'd want for a friend—he looks rather dissipated."

"He was a good man when he worked for Mr. Endicott. But he's not so good since he went over to Merwell."

There the talk about Hank Snogger ended. Once or twice the man looked curiously at Dave.

Each time something in his face struck the youth as decidedly familiar. Yet, try his best, the boy could not place the fellow.

"It's no use," he told himself at last. "Perhaps I don't know him, after all. But I've seen a face like that somewhere—I am sure of it."

CHAPTER XV

AMONG THE COWBOYS

"Here she comes!"

It was an enthusiastic cowboy who uttered the words, and by way of emphasis he fired his revolver in the air, as he rode up beside the incoming train. It was the one moment of excitement at the station.

The cars came to a halt, and Sid Todd went forward to give his letters to the railway mail clerk. Dave watched the cars and saw two men and a boy alight. The boy was Link Merwell.

The former bully of Oak Hall looked haggard, as if his dissipation in Chicago and elsewhere had done him much harm. His eyes were heavy as he stood and stared about him. Hank Snogger had gone forward, to care for the mail from the Merwell ranch.

"Hello, you here!" cried Link, stepping forward and confronting Dave.

"I am," was the cool answer.

"Got here ahead of me, eh?"

"So it would seem."

"Going to make a spread out here, I suppose," went on Link, with a sneer. "Paint the plains red, and all that."

"I came for a good time, but I don't intend to paint anything red."

"Bah, I know you, Dave Porter! You want to crow over everybody, no matter where you go. But you'll find things are different out here from what they were at Oak Hall," added the bully, significantly. "You can't pull the wool over people's eyes here like you did there."

"I have no more intention of pulling wool than I have of painting anything red," answered Dave, as calmly as before. He could see that Link was in a bad humor and spoiling for a fight.

"I said I was going to get square with you, and I am," continued the bully, loudly.

"You keep your distance, Link Merwell," answered Dave, and now his tone was sharper. "Don't forget what I did at Oak Hall. If you want another thrashing like that I can give it to you."

"Get out! Don't you talk to me!" howled Link. "You attacked me when I was sick!" He spoke in a loud voice, for the benefit of the cowboys and others who were gathering around. The train had started away and was soon out of sight among the hills.

"You were as well as you ever were," answered Dave.

"What's the row, Link?" asked Hank Snogger, as he pushed his way to the front.

"Here's a fellow used to go to school with me. I've got it in for him, and I've a good mind to give him a thrashing."

"You put your hand on me, and you'll take the consequences," said Dave. "I didn't come here to fight, but I can defend myself."

"You don't want to fight, do you, Dave?" asked Sid Todd, in a low voice. To him it looked as if the Crumville lad might be no match for Merwell, who was larger and heavier.

"I am not afraid, Todd. I thrashed him once and I can do it again—if I have to."

"You licked him?"

"Yes."

"With your fists?"

"Yes."

"Where?"

"At school. He played a dirty trick on me and some others, and I wouldn't stand for it."

"You shut your mouth!" roared Link Merwell, and without warning he rushed forward and struck Dave a blow in the chest that sent the Crumville youth staggering against Mr. Hooper.

"Wait! wait! This won't do!" said the ranchman.

"If you are going to fight, fight fair," put in Sid Todd.

"Now don't you butt in here, Sid!" growled Hank Snogger, with an ugly look at the other cowboy.

"I'll see fair play," answered Todd, sharply, and he elbowed his way between Snogger and Dave.

Having delivered his unexpected blow, Link Merwell sprang back and stood on the defensive. Dave was not wearing any coat or vest, and he merely threw his hat to his friend. Then, as quick as lightning, he sprang forward, knocked aside Merwell's guard, and planted a telling blow on the bully's left eye.

"As you are so anxious to fight, take that!" cried Dave, and before the other could recover he landed a second blow on Merwell's chin. This caused the bully to stagger against Hank Snogger, who kept him from falling completely.

"Well! well! well!" sang out one of the cowboys in the crowd. "Just look at that! Merwell, keep your eyes open, or you'll git knocked into a jelly!"

The former bully of Oak Hall was staggered, but only for a moment. Then, with a hoarse cry of rage, he leaped at Dave, and for fully a minute the blows came thick and fast from each side. Then the pair clinched, swung around and around, and finally went down, with Dave on top.

"Break away there!" sang out Hank Snogger, and caught Dave by the ear. "Git up off him!"

"Leave Porter alone!" yelled Sid Todd, and caught Snogger by the hair. "This is the boys' fight, 'tain't yours."

"That's right! That's right!" came from several. "Leave the kids alone."

"He ain't goin' to hit Link when he's down," growled Snogger.

"I don't intend to," answered Dave, and got up. He turned to Hank Snogger. "You keep your hands off of me," he added, sharply. "This is not your quarrel."

"Ah, don't talk to me," growled the cowboy.

"I will talk to you," went on Dave. "You keep out of this."

Dave stood back, while Link slowly arose to his feet. The bully was somewhat dazed. But there was still a good deal of fight left in him, and suddenly he charged on the Crumville lad, making a heavy swing for Dave's jaw. Dave ducked, and, as Merwell swung around, caught the bully in the right ear. Then he followed the blow by one on the neck and another directly in the mouth. The latter loosened two teeth and sent the bully into the arms of Hank Snogger.

"Well, have you had enough?" asked Dave. He was panting for breath, and his eyes were blazing with determination.

A look full of the bitterest kind of hatred filled the face of Link Merwell, but he was too staggered to attack Dave again. He leaned on Hank Snogger and then turned his face away.

"I say, have you had enough—or do you want another dose?" demanded Dave.

"I'll—fight this out some other time," answered Merwell, weakly. He realized that the eyes of the crowd were on him, and this made him furious. But he did not dare to risk another attack from the Crumville youth, fearing what fighters call "a knockout."

"Then you have had enough, eh?" went on Dave. "Very well. And now, Merwell, I advise you to keep your distance. If you don't—well, you'll catch it worse, that's all."

"Link is tired out from his long train ride," remarked Hank Snogger. "He ain't in no fit condition fer a scrap. Wait till he has rested up a week or two—then he'll show thet tenderfoot what's what." And with these words he led Link away to where a couple of horses were tied. He leaped on one and the bully leaped on the other, and in a moment more both were off for the Merwell ranch.

"Well, youngster, I reckon you can hold your own," remarked Mr. Hooper. He had led a rough-and-tumble life himself and did not look on a fight as a dreadful matter. "You had him going."

"So you did, Dave," added Sid Todd, while several other cowboys nodded in assent.

"He forced the fight," answered Dave. "I suppose he'll try it again some day."

"Merwell always was scrappy," said one of the cowboys.

"Takes after his dad," added another; and then there was a general laugh. Several came up to shake hands with Dave and congratulate him on the outcome of the little bout. Some of the cowboys were not very refined, and to them such a fist-fight seemed a great thing.

There were a number of letters for those at Star Ranch, including two for Dave,—from his father and from Ben Basswood. With the epistles in their pockets, Dave and Sid Todd started on the return to the Endicott place. They had to follow, for some distance, the trail taken by Link and Snogger, their road branching off after the bridge over the river was crossed.

Considerable time had been lost waiting for the train and because of the set-to with Merwell, and the sun was now going down over the mountains in the west, casting long shadows over the plains.

"You'll have a late supper to-night," said Todd, as they moved on at a brisk pace. "And I reckon you'll have an appetite for it. The way you polished off that cub was great!" And he shook his head enthusiastically.

"I wish you'd do me a favor, Todd," returned Dave.

"Sure thing, son. What do you want?"

"Please don't say too much at the ranch about the fight. I don't want to scare my sister and the other girls."

"Can't I tell the boys how you polished off young Merwell? Most of 'em will be glad to hear it."

"Well, don't say too much, that's all. If they learn that Link is on the watch to do harm, the girls will be almost too afraid to go out."

"Do you think that cub would be mean enough to harm the gals?"

"He'd be mean enough to scare them half to death."

"If he does that—well, I reckon I'll take a hand in lickin' him myself."

"We came out here to have a good time, and I want to forget Link Merwell, if possible. But I'll keep my eyes open for him—and I'll tell Phil and Roger to watch out, too," added Dave, soberly.

Sid Todd was anxious to know more of Link's doings at Oak Hall, and Dave told how Link had tried to get Gus Plum and himself into trouble. He did not mention the trouble Laura and Jessie had had, for he did not wish to drag the names of the girls into the affair.

"He sure is a bad egg," said the cowboy, at the end of the recital. "Keep an eye on him by all means."

By the time they reached the vicinity of the bridge it was quite dark. Remembering the bad condition of the structure spanning the stream, Sid Todd cautioned Dave to let his horse walk.

"Look!" cried the youth, a second later, and pointed around a rise of rocks to the bridge. He had seen two figures leaving the structure. They disappeared behind a high clump of brushwood.

"What did you see?" questioned Todd, who had been gazing off to one side of the trail.

"Two persons on the bridge. They just ran away into the bushes."

"On foot?"

"Yes."

"Humph! Didn't know anybody was out on foot around here," mused the cowboy. "Sure it wasn't a bear, or some other animal?" And he felt for his horse-pistol.

"No, they were men, or boys," answered Dave. "They ran off the bridge the minute we came in sight."

"Huh! I wonder if it's possible them hoss-thieves is around again."

"Have you horse-thieves in this territory?"

"We sure have. Lost two hosses last spring and two last summer. I'll have to tell the boss about seeing them fellows. But maybe—say, hold on, Dave."

"What now?"

"I may be mistaken, but—don't go on the bridge on hossback."

"Why not?"

"I'll tell you—after I've examined the bridge," answered Sid Todd, and in a manner that mystified Dave very much.

CHAPTER XVI

A MEETING ON THE TRAIL

Arriving at the bridge, Sid Todd told Dave to halt, and the pair dismounted. As they did so they heard a sound in the bushes beside the stream. They looked in the direction, but saw nobody.

The cowboy had drawn his pistol, and with this in hand he walked closer to the bridge. His eyes were on the planking, and presently he uttered an exclamation:

"The rascals!"

He pointed to two of the planks, and Dave saw that they were loose and so placed that the slightest jar would send them down into the stream.

"Do you think those men I just saw did this?" questioned Dave.

"Certainly they did! They ought to be hung for it, too!" answered the cowboy, wrathfully.

"But what for—to cripple our horses?"

"Either that, or to cripple us. Dave, we've got to be on our guard. If those hoss-thieves are watching us—"

"I don't think they were horse-thieves, Todd."

"You don't? Then—" The cowboy broke off into a low whistle. "Do you mean to say Link Merwell would play such a dirty trick?"

"Yes, I do. You haven't any idea how that fellow hates me."

"Hum!" mused Sid Todd. "Well, maybe, but I thought it must be the hoss-thieves."

"Why would horse-thieves want to hurt our horses?"

"They wouldn't want to do that, but they might be thinking our horses would fall and throw us. But I see that reasoning is weak. Maybe it was young Merwell—and Hank Snogger. If it was, they ought to be punished good an' proper, hear me!" went on the cowboy, with emphasis.

"I am going to look around the bushes," went on Dave, determinedly.

"Look out that you don't get into trouble, son. Anybody who would do this would do worse."

Dave had seen a heavy stick lying beside the road, and arming himself with this, he walked to the bushes and around them. In the soft soil he made out a number of hoof-prints, and he called Todd's attention to these.

"On hossback, both of 'em," said the cowboy, after an examination. "Dave, you was right," he announced, a little later. "It must have been Merwell and Snogger, fer see, they have taken the old trail along the river. That leads to another trail that runs to the Merwell ranch."

"Well, they are gone, that's certain," answered the youth, after another look around. "We may as well be on our way. But we ought to mend the bridge."

"We'll do that,—an' post a warning, too," said the cowboy.

Not without difficulty, they managed to fasten the planks into place once more. Then, at either end of the rickety structure, they set up a stick in the road.

"That's the usual warning in this country," explained Todd. "It means 'Go slow and look out.'"

When the pair arrived at Star Ranch they found the boys and girls waiting for them.

"You must have walked back," said Belle. "We have been waiting for you ever since we heard the locomotive whistle."

"Oh, we had to stop to fix the bridge," answered Dave, and then handed around the letters, which instantly claimed attention, so no more questions were asked. Then the Crumville youth had supper, and by that time it was late enough to go to bed.

"You've got a cut on your cheek, Dave," said Phil, when the three boys were undressing. "Did you scratch yourself?"

"Thereby hangs a tale, Phil," quoted Dave, and then, in a low voice, told of the encounter at the railroad station, and gave the true particulars of the trouble at the river.

"It's the same old Link!" murmured Roger. "We'll have to watch out for him!"

"I really think the girls ought to be warned," said Phil. "There is no telling what mean thing Link might do—if he met them alone."

"Well, we don't want to frighten them," answered Dave.

"Better frighten them than give Link the chance to annoy them," answered the senator's son.

"Say, I wish I had seen you polish off Link!" cried Phil. "It would have done my heart good. I'll wager he was as mad as he could be!"

"Oh, he was mad enough," replied Dave, with a grim smile. "But say, when you get the chance, I want you to look at that Hank Snogger. He looks like somebody I've met somewhere, but for the life of me I can't place him."

"Is he handsome?" quizzed the shipowner's son.

"No, he looks melancholy—as if he had something on his mind. It's a peculiar face, and for the life of me I can't get it out of my mind."

Several days passed and nothing of importance happened. The boys and girls enjoyed themselves thoroughly, and the Endicotts did all in their power to make the visitors feel at home. At first, Jessie was inclined to be a little shy, but soon this wore away and she felt as happy as anybody.

"It certainly is a splendid spot," said she to Dave. "I don't wonder Laura was anxious to get back, and to have you see it."

"It suits me—I wouldn't ask for a better vacation, especially"—Dave dropped his voice a little—"with you along, Jessie."

"Oh, Dave!" she cried, and blushed.

"It wouldn't be half so much fun if you hadn't come along, Jessie," he went on. "I am very, very glad that we are here—together."

"Well, so—so am I," answered the girl, and then, still blushing, she ran off to join Belle and Laura. But the look she gave Dave warmed his heart as it had never been warmed before.

Sunday passed, with a little home service, in which all those in the house and also a few of the cowboys joined. The boys and girls sang some of the familiar church songs, and this the cowboys greatly enjoyed.

"We don't git much in the way of entertainment here," explained Sid Todd, "and that singin' sounds mighty good to us. It touches a fellow here, too," he added, with his finger over his heart.

"If Mr. Endicott will permit it, we'll give you boys an entertainment before we go home," answered Dave. "We give them at Oak Hall, you know,—and the girls can help."

"Say, that sure would be fine!" answered the cowboy, enthusiastically.

The boys had found out from Mr. Endicott where good fishing could be had, and early of the second week at Star Ranch they went out, taking the girls with them. All were on horseback, and carried lunch along, for they were to remain out all day.

"Now keep out of trouble," said Mrs. Endicott, as they rode away. "And be sure to come back before dark."

"We'll be back by six, mamma," answered Belle. "And you needn't worry about us, for we'll be perfectly safe."

They were bound for a spot among the foothills, about six miles away. Here was located a mountain torrent, said to be filled with the gamiest kind of specimens of the finny tribe. Sid Todd had told them of a particularly good bend in the stream, where fishing was bound to be excellent, and Belle said she knew the trail, having gone to the locality several times with her father. She was a true young sportswoman, and could fish almost as well as her parent. She carried the same kind of an outfit as did the boys. Jessie and Laura did not expect to fish, but said they would watch the others, and pick wild flowers, and also prepare the lunch when it came time to eat.

All were in the best of health and spirits when they departed. It promised to be an ideal day, with the sun shining clearly, and a gentle breeze blowing from the northwest. They passed along at a smart gait, for the boys and Belle were anxious to try their luck with their lines and poles.

"If we catch enough, right from the start, we can fry some fish for lunch," said Dave. "I love fish just from the water."

"Oh, so do I!" cried Belle. "They seem so much sweeter."

"In the city one gets them all packed in ice, and then half the flavor is gone," added Laura.

They started in a bunch, but gradually drifted into pairs, Dave riding beside Jessie, Roger escorting Laura, and Phil taking the lead with Belle. The senator's son and Dave's sister had become very "chummy," and it can be said that Phil and Belle were fully as attentive to one another as the occasion warranted. All told stories and sang, and the boys whistled.

Half an hour of riding brought them to the edge of a woods, and here they had to proceed in single file, or "Indian fashion," as Belle expressed it.

"By the way, are there any Indians around here?" asked Jessie, timidly.

"A few, and they are very peaceable," answered the ranch owner's daughter. "Our only enemies are the cattle-and horse-thieves."

They were passing through some dense underbrush when Belle suddenly called a halt. The trail was very narrow, and on either side grew dense clumps of trees.

"Somebody is coming," announced the girl.

"On this trail?" asked Laura.

"Yes."

"We'll have some fun passing each other, especially if it's a fat man," remarked Roger, dryly, and this caused a laugh.

They waited, and presently saw a boy approaching on horse-back, followed by a lean-looking man who wore a tattered cowboy dress and a much-battered sombrero.

"It's Link Merwell!" exclaimed Phil.

He was right, and the bully did not stop until his horse stood directly in front of that ridden by Belle. Then he came to a halt, and his companion halted directly behind him.

"I want to pass," growled Link, without so much as raising his hat or bidding the time of day.

"All right, pass," answered Phil, stiffly. "We are not keeping you."

"You are blocking the trail."

"Can't you pass around the ladies?" questioned Roger.

"I've got as much right on this trail as you," returned the bully, shooting a dark look at the others. "You needn't think you own everything!"

"Oh, let us ride to one side and let him pass!" whispered Jessie. "He may want to fight if we don't!"

"He won't fight with so many against him," answered Dave.

"You are very considerate of the ladies, I must say," said Roger. "We'll give you half the trail and no more," and he urged his horse a little to one side and Dave and Phil did the same. The girls moved still further over, so that Link Merwell might not touch them as he passed.

"Where are you going?" demanded the bully, as he moved slowly forward.

"That is our affair, not yours," answered Dave, sharply.

"You keep off my father's land!"

"We don't intend to go near your land," said Belle, coldly.

"Oh, I didn't mean you, Belle, I meant Dave Porter and his cronies."

"Mr. Porter and his friends are my guests, Mr. Merwell. When you insult them, you insult me." And Belle held her head high in the air.

"All right; have your own way, if you want to. I haven't got anything against you and your folks. But I don't intend these outsiders shall ride over me," growled Link. He faced Dave. "I'm not done with you yet, remember that!" he added, bitterly. Then he rode on, and the lean-looking man behind him followed. Belle looked at the man curiously, but the fellow kept his face averted as he slipped by. Soon boy and man had disappeared from view.

"Talk about a lemon!" cried Phil. "Say, isn't Link the sourest ever!"

"He certainly is," answered Roger.

"Let's forget him," said Dave. "We are out for fun to-day, not for trouble." And then they moved forward as before. Little did any of them dream of what that unexpected meeting in the woods was to bring forth.

Edward Stratemeyer

CHAPTER XVII

IN WHICH SOME HORSES ARE STOLEN

A half hour more of riding brought the little party to the bank of the stream at a point where Belle said they would be sure to find good fishing. Here there was something of a pool, the river tumbling from some rocks above. The pool was lined with rocks and brushwood, and behind these was a glade, backed up by the woods.

"What a lovely spot!" cried Jessie, enthusiastically, as Dave assisted her to dismount, and took charge of her horse. "Just look at the wild flowers among the rocks! One would not believe that they could grow in such a place!"

"I am glad I brought my camera with me," said Laura. "I am sure I shall get some fine pictures."

Belle showed the boys where the animals might be tethered, and they took particular care to fasten the steeds properly, as Sid Todd had instructed them. Then they got out their fishing-rods, and also that of Belle, and baited up with the artificial flies they had brought along.

"We'll fish for an hour," announced Dave. "And then I'll knock off and start up a campfire."

"When you do that be careful and not set fire to the woods," said Belle. "Papa is very much afraid of fire."

"I don't blame him," put in Roger. "A fire out here would do a terrible amount of damage."

The boys and Belle were soon busy fishing, in the pool and along the lower part of the river. The stream was about thirty feet in width and from a foot to four foot deep, with great rocks sticking up here and there. Trout and some other fish were plentiful, and all had but little difficulty in getting bites, and it was great sport to play their catches and land them.

"This is the best fishing I ever saw!" cried Phil, as he succeeded in landing an extra fine mountain trout. "I don't wonder that fishermen come many miles to gratify their taste for such sport."

"Here's another!" exclaimed Belle, merrily, and brought in a fish that was a beauty. Roger and Dave both leaped to help her, and soon the catch was dropped into a side pool with the others.

While the boys and Belle were fishing, Laura and Jessie wandered up and down the rocks and the grassy glade beyond, gathering wild flowers and also some blackberries that grew in that vicinity. Dave's sister also succeeded in getting several photographs, including two of the others with their fishing outfits.

"Now, I want you all to stand in a group, with your fish on strings," said Laura, a little later, when the fishing seemed to slow up a little. And then she arranged them to suit herself and took two snapshots.

"Now, let me take a snapshot of you and Jessie, with your bunches of wild flowers," said Dave, and this was soon added to the other films.

They had great fun building a campfire and preparing lunch. The boys cut the wood and started the blaze, and even made coffee, while the girls spread a tablecloth that had been brought along, and put out tin plates and tin cups, and the various good things to eat. Then some of the fish were cleaned by the boys and fried by the girls, and all sat down to enjoy what every one declared was better than a feast at a hotel. In the meantime the horses were tethered in a new place, so that they could crop the luxurious grass.

"I can tell you one thing, life in the open air gives one a great appetite," remarked the senator's son, as he smacked his lips over a particularly dainty portion of trout.

"As if there was ever anything the matter with Roger's appetite," cried Phil.

"How about yourself, Phil?" questioned Dave, with a grin.

"Oh, I reckon I can get away with my share," answered the shipowner's son calmly, as he reached for another portion of the fish.

As there was no hurry, the boys and girls took their time over the meal, and many were the stories told and the jokes cracked while the food was disappearing.

"If only some of the Oak Hall boys could see us now!" cried Dave. "Wouldn't they envy us!"

"They certainly would," answered Roger.

"And what of the girls at home?" asked Jessie. "I rather think they'd like to be in our place."

"Crumville seems a long way off, doesn't it?" said Laura.

Besides the fish, they had chicken sandwiches, cake, pie, and half a dozen other things to eat, and coffee, and water from a sparkling spring to drink. When they had finished, they took it easy for a while, and then fished some more, and went strolling.

"I think we had better be thinking of returning," said Belle, at length. "It is a long ride back, remember, and unless I am mistaken there is a storm coming up."

"A storm!" cried Jessie. "Oh, I hope not!"

"We don't want to get wet," added Laura.

"I don't think the storm will come right away. But I don't like the looks of the clouds yonder."

"They certainly do look bad," remarked Dave, casting his eyes in the direction to which Belle pointed. "It didn't look like rain this morning."

"It may be more wind than rain, Dave. Sometimes we have great windstorms around Star Ranch."

They were quite a distance up the river shore when Belle called attention to the clouds. They had gone up to get a view of a small but picturesque waterfall, and Laura had taken several snapshots, with the boys and girls in the foreground, seated on a fallen tree trunk. Now all started back in the direction of the temporary camp.

"Say, Roger, you help the girls pack up," said Dave. "Phil and I can get the horses ready. Be sure to see that the fire is out, too," he called back.

"All right," answered the senator's son. "The fire is out—I saw to that before," he added.

The horses had been tethered at some distance from the camping-out spot, behind some heavy brushwood, where the grass was extra thick and nutritious. Dave hurried in that direction, with Phil at his heels.

When the two youths reached the spot, both stared around in perplexity.

"Why, Dave—" stammered the shipowner's son. "I thought—"

"We left the horses here!" cried Dave. "I'm sure of it."

"Then where are they now?"

"Maybe they broke loose and wandered away."

"Or else they have been stolen!"

"Stolen!"

"Yes,—it couldn't be otherwise. They wandered away or they have been stolen."

"We'll take a look around."

Both boys hurried, first in one direction, and then another. They could see hoof-prints in the grass, leading towards the rocks back of the bushes, but that was all. The horses had been tethered to some saplings.

"The halters didn't break, that's certain," said Phil, soberly. "For if they did, we'd find the broken ends."

"I can't understand it," returned Dave, and his face grew thoughtful.

"Hello!" came in Roger's voice. "Why don't you bring those horses? We are all ready to go."

"Come here!" called back Dave. "Something is wrong!"

The senator's son answered the summons on a run, and the three girls trailed behind him. The newcomers to Star Ranch did not know what to say, but Belle uttered a cry of dismay:

"Horse-thieves!"

"Oh, Belle, do you really think somebody has stolen the horses?" queried Laura, while Jessie turned very pale.

"Yes, I do," was the blunt response. "That is, if they were tied properly."

"Yes, they were well tied—I saw to that myself," said Dave.

"I know mine was tied fast, and so was Laura's," added the senator's son.

"And I put a double knot in the rope to Belle's and mine," came from Phil.

"One thing is sure," said Laura. "They couldn't very well all break away at once."

"I am sure it is the work of horse-thieves," responded Belle. "Papa has been afraid they might come back."

"But how did they know about our horses being here?" asked Phil.

"They must have watched us and seen us ride away from the ranch, and then they followed, and took the horses while we were up the river."

"If only we could follow them, and get the horses back!" said the senator's son, with a sigh.

"They must be worth a lot of money," murmured Jessie. "Oh, supposing they had shot us!" she added, tremblingly.

"Horse-thieves are usually cowards," answered Belle. "They won't shoot unless they are cornered. I'd like to follow them myself, but we can't do it on foot."

"What are we to do?" asked Laura, and looked at her brother.

"I don't know," answered Dave. "One or two of us boys might walk back to the ranch and tell the folks of what has happened."

"But it is such a distance, Dave!" cried Jessie. "And see how black the sky is getting!" she added.

"It is quite a number of miles to the ranch house," said Belle. "You would not be able to reach there until long after nightfall."

"I shouldn't mind that," answered Dave. "But what will the rest of you do in the meantime? You can't stay out here in the open very well, with that storm coming on."

"Dave, you're not going to the house alone," cried Laura. "I'll not allow it. Supposing those horse-thieves should be watching you? They might attack you, and rob you!"

"Yes, please don't think of going alone," pleaded Jessie, and her eyes began to fill with tears.

"Dave is not going alone. I am going with him," declared Roger.

"No, I'll go," volunteered Phil. "You can stay with the girls."

"Well, both of you can't go," answered Dave, with a grim smile. "Somebody has got to stay here,—in fact, I think it would be better that both of you stay with the girls—in case I don't get back with help by morning."

"Of course, if it wasn't for the loss of the horses we could all stay here," said Belle. "Papa will be sure to send somebody out to look us up when it gets late and we are not back. But I think he ought to know about the horses just as soon as possible."

"Is there any sort of a shelter around here?" questioned Roger.

"Yes, there is a shack about a quarter of a mile up the river," answered the ranch owner's daughter. "Papa stayed there several nights, once upon a time. It isn't much of a place, but it will shelter us from the storm."

"Are you sure you can find it?"

"Oh, yes, I've been there twice."

"Then you and the others had best put up there for the night, and I'll start at once for the ranch house," went on Dave. "I am not afraid, and I'll keep my eyes wide open for those horse-thieves," he continued.

But to this plan the girls would not listen, and at last it was arranged that Roger should remain with the girls, while Dave and Phil walked to the house for aid. The crowd left behind were to hurry to the shack up the river, and there make themselves as comfortable as possible until help arrived.

"Do be careful now, Dave!" said his sister, as he was on the point of departing.

"Yes! yes!" added Jessie. "I shall worry every minute until you get back!"

"Don't be alarmed," answered Dave. "We'll get through all right, and have help here before you know it."

"Are you sure of the trail?" asked Belle.

"Oh, yes, that's easy," answered Phil.

Without another word the two chums started off in the direction of the ranch house, so many miles distant. The others, watched them out of sight, and then turned and walked up the river bank toward the shack Belle had mentioned.

CHAPTER XVIII

OUT IN THE WIND AND RAIN

"Dave, what do you suppose those six horses were worth?" questioned Phil, as the two youths hurried along the back trail on a dog-trot,—the same dog-trot they used when on a cross-country run at Oak Hall.

"At least two thousand dollars, Phil," was the reply. "The horse I used was a dandy, and so was that Belle had—and yours was a good one, too."

"What do you suppose those horse-thieves will do with them?"

"Drive them a long distance, hide them for a while, and then, when they get the chance, sell them. Of course they don't expect to get full value for them, but they'll get a neat sum."

"You don't suppose this can be a trick of Link Merwell's?"

"I thought of that, but I don't think so. Taking a horse in this section of the country is a serious business. Why, they used to hang horse-thieves, and even now a ranchman wouldn't hesitate to shoot at a fellow who had his horse and was making off with it. No, I don't think Link would quite dare to play such a trick. But of course we can investigate,—after we have reported to Mr. Endicott."

"You are not going to try to keep up this dog-trot all the way to the house, are you?" questioned the shipowner's son, after about a mile had been covered, and when they were passing over a rather rough portion of the trail.

"Winded?"

"Not exactly, but I shall be if I keep this up," panted Phil. "Besides, I don't want to tumble over these tree roots."

"I wanted to get as far as possible on the way before that storm broke," went on Dave, glancing anxiously upward, between the branches of the trees. "When it comes, I rather think it will be a corker. I hope the others reach that shack before it rains."

"Oh, they ought to be there by this time."

The boys kept on, sometimes running and sometimes dropping into a walk. As they advanced, the sky kept growing steadily darker, both on account of the storm and because the day was drawing to a close.

"Here's the spot where we passed Link and that man with him," said Dave, presently. "Wonder who that fellow was?"

"Oh, some hand from the Merwell ranch, I suppose. He didn't seem to be very sociable. He kept his head turned away all the time Link was talking to us."

"If he's from the Merwell place, they can't have very nice fellows up there."

"Well, who would want to work for a man like Mr. Merwell? He and Link are just alike, dictatorial and mean."

The two boys kept on for a short distance further. Then Phil caught his foot in a tree root and went sprawling.

"Wow!" he spluttered, as he arose. "Hi, Dave, wait for me!" he added, for his chum had continued on the run.

"What's wrong?"

"I tripped and fell—just as I was afraid I'd do. Better go slow—unless you want to break an ankle or skin your nose."

"The storm is coming," said Dave, as he came to a stop. "Much hurt?"

"Not very,—scratched my hand, that's all. Phew! listen to the wind!"

The sky overhead was black with clouds, but to the north and the south were great patches of light. The wind was increasing steadily.

"Maybe it will be more wind than rain," said Dave. "I hope so, too, for I have no fancy for getting drenched to the skin."

"I don't like a wind storm—when I am in a big woods like this," answered the shipowner's son. "I am always afraid a tree will come down on me."

"Well, we have got to look out for that—if we can," answered Dave, gravely. "I don't like it myself, but it can't be helped."

They continued on their way. The wind increased rapidly, and soon it grew so dark they could see little or nothing under the thickest of the trees. They came to an open space, and there the wind struck them with great force, almost hurling them flat.

"Say, I think—we had—had better wait a—a bit!" panted Phil, as he clutched Dave by the arm.

"Let us get over to yonder rocks," answered Dave. "We'll be a little safer there than between the trees."

Hand in hand the chums crossed the glade and made for a series of rocks looming between the trees beyond. The wind was now blowing with almost tornado force, and with it came a few scattering drops of rain. Just as they gained the rocks something whizzed past their heads.

"What was that?" gasped Phil, ducking after the object had passed.

"It was a small tree limb," answered Dave. "We've got to watch out. Hark!"

They listened, and above the whistling of the wind heard a great crash.

"It's a tree being blown down!" cried Phil. "Come on, let us get between the rocks, before something hits us on the head!"

Much alarmed, both boys leaped for the shelter of the rocks, and in the darkness felt their way until they reached a split that was seven or eight feet deep and a foot wide at the bottom and twice that at the top.

"I guess this is as good a place as any, Phil," remarked Dave, when he had regained his breath sufficiently to speak.

"It won't be much protection if it rains hard," grumbled the shipowner's son.

"Well, I don't see that we can do better."

"Neither do I."

Further conversation was cut off by the wind and the rain. The former shrieked and whistled through the woods, sending down branch after branch with tremendous crashes that awed the boys completely. The rain was light, but the drops were large and hit them with stinging force.

For fully half an hour the blow continued, and then it appeared to let up and the rain stopped entirely.

"Shall we go on?" questioned Phil, standing up and trying to pierce the darkness around them.

"Better hold up a while, Phil," answered Dave. "This is as safe a spot as any, with the wind blowing down the trees all around us."

They waited, and it was well that they did so, for presently the wind started to whistle once more, growing louder and louder. A small tree branch came down on them, and then came a crash that made them both jump.

"It's coming this way!" yelled Phil. "The tree behind the rocks!"

"Get down!" cried Dave, and threw himself flat.

Both boys crouched as low as possible. They heard the tree bend and crack. Then came a tremendous crash, and they felt one of the rocks moving.

"Maybe we'll be crushed to a jelly!" groaned the shipowner's son.

There was no time to say more, for an instant later the tree came down, directly over the top of the opening. Several small branches thrust themselves down upon the lads, pinning them to the bottom of the crevice. The rocks trembled, and for the moment the boys were afraid they would be crushed to death, as Phil had intimated.

"Safe, Phil?" asked Dave, as the rocking of the stones and the big tree ceased and the wind seemed to die down once more.

"I—I guess so! A tree limb is on my back, though."

"I've got one across my legs."

With caution both boys crawled from beneath the branches

and out of the split in the rocks. They could see where the big tree had been uprooted, leaving a hole in the soil fifteen feet in diameter. The top of the tree was all of a hundred feet away from this hole.

"We were lucky to be between the rocks, Phil," said Dave, with a grave shake of his head. "Otherwise, if that tree had come down on us—"

"We wouldn't be here to tell the tale," finished the shipowner's son. "Ugh! it makes me shiver to look at it."

"Now it is down, we may as well get between the rocks until we are sure this blow is over," went on Dave, after standing several minutes in the rain.

This appeared the best thing to do, and they crawled back into the crevice and partly under the tree. Here the thick branches protected the lads, so that but little rain reached them.

A dismal hour went by, and then the storm came to an end. The wind died down into a gentle breeze and the rain was reduced to a few scattering drops, to which they paid no attention.

"If only that wind didn't blow the shack down on the other folks' heads," said Dave. He was thinking of how frightened the girls, and especially Jessie, must have been.

"I'll wager the trail is now a mass of mud and water," said Phil, and he was right, and as they progressed, they frequently got into the mud up to their ankles.

It was eleven o'clock when they gained the edge of the woods and came out on the plains. The sky was still overcast, only a few stars being faintly visible.

"Are you sure of the right direction, Dave?" asked the shipowner's son, as both paused to look around.

"I think this is the trail, Phil, don't you?" and Dave pointed with his finger to a deep rut in the soil.

"Yes. But that doesn't make it right," and Phil gazed around in some perplexity.

"What do you mean? This is the only trail around here."

"So I see. But, somehow, this edge of the woods doesn't look familiar to me. I thought we entered at a point where I saw a clump of four trees on the left."

"Hum! I rather think I saw those trees myself," mused Dave. "But I don't see them now."

"Neither do I, and that makes me think that perhaps we came out of the woods at the wrong spot."

Much perplexed, the two lads walked around the edge of the woods for a considerable distance. But they saw nothing of any other trail and so came back to the point from which they had started.

"This must be right, after all," was Phil's comment. "Anyway, it's the only trail here, so we may as well follow it."

They hurried on, the halt under the rocks having rested them a good deal. Out on the prairie the trail grew a bit drier, for which they were thankful. They got into their dog-trot once more, and thus covered all of two miles in a short space of time. Then, of a sudden, both came to a halt in dismay.

"Which one?" asked Phil, laconically.

"Don't know," was Dave's equally laconic answer.

Before them the trail branched out in three different directions, like three spokes within the right angle of a wheel.

"This is a regular Chinese puzzle," said Dave, after an inspection of the trails. "The one to the right looks to be the most traveled."

The two boys made every possible effort to pierce the darkness ahead of them, and presently Phil fancied he saw a light in the distance. Dave was not sure if it was a light or a star just showing above the clearing horizon.

"Well, we may as well go ahead," said the shipowner's son. "No use in staying here trying to figure it out."

They went on, taking the center one of the three trails. They had covered less than quarter of a mile when Phil gave a shout.

"It is a light, I am sure of it—the light of a lamp or lantern! Hurrah! we must be on the right trail after all!"

"Go slow, Phil," cried Dave, a sudden thought striking him. "That may not be a ranch light."

"Yes, but—"

"It may be something much worse—for us."

"What do you mean?"

"It may be the light from the camp of the horse-thieves."

CHAPTER XIX

A FRUITLESS SEARCH

Phil stared at Dave in consternation.

"Do you really think that?" he cried.

"I don't say I think so, I only say it may be," returned the youth from Crumville.

"If they are the horse-thieves, and we watch our chances, we may get the animals back!"

"Not unless it is a single thief, Phil. We don't want to run the risk of getting shot in the dark."

"That's true."

With great caution the two lads advanced along the muddy trail. As they got closer to the light they saw that it came from a log house, low and rambling. Not far away were several other buildings, and also a corral.

"We are on the right trail after all!" sang out the shipowner's son, joyfully, and commenced to run at the best speed he could command.

"Hold on!" called Dave, but Phil was so eager to get to the house first that he paid no attention to the words. Not until he had reached the very piazza of the building did he pause to stare around him.

"Why, it's not Mr. Endicott's place at all!" he exclaimed.

He had made considerable noise ascending the piazza, and now a door was flung open, letting a stream of light flood his face, momentarily blinding him.

"Hello! what do you want?" demanded a man Phil had never seen before.

"Why—er—what place is this?" stammered the youth, and as he asked the question Dave came up behind him.

"This is the Triple X Ranch," was the man's answer.

"What! Mr. Merwell's place?" stammered Phil.

"That's it. Want to see him? Why, say, you're all out of wind,—anything wrong?"

"I—I didn't know this was the Merwell place," murmured Phil. He knew not what else to say, he was so taken back.

"Who is that, Jerry?" asked another voice, and a moment later Felix Merwell stepped into view. As he saw Dave he scowled slightly.

"Why, Mr. Merwell, we—er—" commenced Phil, and then he looked at Dave.

"We were out and we lost our way in the darkness and got on the wrong trail," said Dave, quickly. "Will you be kind enough to direct us to the trail to Mr. Endicott's ranch?"

"Endicott's ranch is a good bit from here," growled Felix Merwell.

"But, Dave—" interrupted Phil, when a meaning look from his chum silenced him.

"Haven't you got no hosses?" asked the man who had first come to the door.

"No, but we don't mind that," said Dave. "We can walk."

"Jerry, show them the trail," said Mr. Merwell, shortly, and turned his back on the boys.

The ranch hand came out without waiting to get his hat or coat, and walked to a point back of the corral.

"It's a long, lonely way," he said, kindly. "You ought to have horses."

"How many miles?" asked Dave.

"About one and a half."

"Oh, that is not so far."

"Got caught in the storm, eh?"

"Yes."

"Link is out too and the old man is kind of worried about him. He sent Hank Snogger out to look for him."

"Then Link didn't come back this afternoon?" said Dave, quickly.

"No, he's been out since early morning. You met him, eh?"

"Yes, but that was about the middle of the forenoon. He was over in the woods."

"It was such a blow the old man is worried, thinking Link

might have got caught under a tree in the woods, or something like that. There's your trail. Keep to that and it will take you right to the Endicott corral."

"Thank you," said both boys, and a moment later they and the man had separated. The ranch hand watched them out of sight, then returned to the house.

"Dave, why didn't you tell them about the horse-thieves?" asked Phil, as soon as he deemed it safe to ask the question.

"I didn't want to ask any favors of Mr. Merwell, that's why," was the reply. "I don't believe he'd want to go after them, and I didn't want to borrow any horses from him."

"Well, I don't blame you for looking at it that way. But we may be losing valuable time."

"We ought to be able to reach Mr. Endicott's place inside of twenty minutes. Come on," and Dave increased his speed.

"Did you note the fact that Link has not yet returned?" said the shipowner's son.

"Yes, but that doesn't prove anything. He may have crept into some place for shelter from the storm, just as we did."

The two youths kept on steadily and before long saw another light in the distance. Then they heard hoofbeats, and soon several forms on horseback loomed out of the darkness.

"Hello!" sang out the voice of Sid Todd. "Who are you?"

"Todd!" called Dave, and a moment later the cowboy rode up, followed by another ranch hand and Mr. Endicott.

"What is wrong?" demanded the railroad president, quickly. "Where are the others?" and his face showed his extreme anxiety.

"The others are safe, so far as we know," answered Dave. "But we have had quite an adventure." And then he and Phil told of how the horses had been stolen, and of how they themselves had been caught in the woods during the great blow.

"The horse-thieves again!" exclaimed Mr. Endicott, wrathfully. "We must get after them this time and run them down! Todd, tell the other men at once! We must lose no time in getting after them! And send word around to the other ranches!"

The railroad president smiled grimly when the boys told him of the brief stop at the Merwell place.

"I don't blame you for not wanting aid from Mr. Merwell," said he. "I want to leave him alone myself. I am only sorry I have him for a neighbor. I'd help him to sell out, if he wished to do so."

The boys went to the house and were speedily given something to eat,—for they had had nothing since noon. They also donned some dry clothing.

"It won't do any good for you to go out again," said Mr. Endicott. "I'll go out, and so will most of the hands. You can remain here with Mrs. Endicott, who is very nervous because of the storm and the absence of Belle."

"As you think best, sir," answered Dave; and so it was arranged. Truth to tell, both Dave and Phil were glad to rest, for the long walk and the experience in the woods during the storm had tired them greatly. Each threw himself on a couch, and almost before he knew it was sound asleep.

When the two boys awoke it was morning. They found that Mrs. Endicott had covered them up with light blankets. A sound outside had aroused them.

It was the other young people returning, on horses Sid Todd had taken to them. Dave and Phil sprang up to meet them.

"Oh, I am so glad to get back!" cried Belle, as she ran to embrace her mother. "Such a time as we have had!"

"Oh, yes, we were safe enough, after we got to the shack," said Laura, in answer to a question from her brother. "But, oh, how it did blow!"

"We were afraid the shack would be carried right up into the air," said Jessie. "And we were so worried about you—thinking a tree in the woods would come down on you."

"Well, one did, pretty nearly," answered Dave, and gave the particulars.

"The men have all gone off after the horse-thieves," said Roger. "But Todd hasn't much hope of tracing them, for the rain washed out all the hoofmarks."

The newcomers were tremendously hungry, and a hearty meal was gotten ready with all the speed of which the Chinese cook was capable. As they ate, the boys and girls told the details of their experience at the shack up the river.

"Did you see anything more of Link or that man with him?" asked Dave.

"No," answered the senator's son. "We've been wondering if they had anything to do with the disappearance of the horses."

"We have been wondering the same thing," said Phil.

"I spoke to papa about it, and he says he will interview Mr. Merwell—if they get no trace of the thieves," said the ranch owner's daughter.

Those who had been at the shack all night were so tired that they went to bed directly after eating, and Dave and Phil were glad enough to rest some more; so that the balance of the day passed quietly. It was not until after sundown that Mr.

Endicott showed himself, followed by about half of the ranch hands.

"We thought we found the trail, but we lost it again," said the ranch owner. "Todd and some of the others are still at it, but I am afraid the thieves are out of our reach. I have sent word to the sheriff, and I suppose he'll put some men on the trail to-morrow."

"Did you stop at the Merwell ranch?" asked Belle.

"Yes, I stopped there less than an hour ago. Mr. Merwell had just come in from a hunt for Link."

"What! then Link isn't back yet?" cried Dave.

"No, and his father was a good deal worried about his absence. When I told about the loss of the horses, Mr. Merwell was worried more yet. He said we needn't think that his son touched them."

"It is queer where Link is keeping himself," mused Roger.

"That's true—unless he was hurt by the storm," answered Phil.

"Have you any idea who these horse-thieves are?" asked Dave.

"We have a general idea, yes," answered Mr. Endicott. "The gang who took the other animals was led by a bold cowboy named Andy Andrews. Andrews is a thoroughly bad egg, and there had been a reward offered for his capture for several years. More than likely this raid was made by him or under his directions."

"Then I sincerely hope they round up this Andy Andrews," remarked Dave.

"So do I—and that we get our horses back."

The night and the next day passed quietly. When it grew dark Sid Todd came in, followed by several of the ranch hands. The look on the foreman's face showed that he had had no success in his hunt.

"We got the trail once, but lost it ag'in," said the cowboy. "The sheriff has got a posse of six men working on the trail now,—but I don't think they'll make anything out of it." And then he told the story of how the woods had been scoured, and of a hunt along the river and over the plains. The men had ridden many miles and were all but exhausted.

"Did you see anybody from the Merwell ranch?" asked Dave.

"Saw Link and his father just as we were coming home," answered Sid Todd. "Merwell said he had seen nothing of the thieves."

"Did Link say anything?"

"No. He was dead tired and he looked scared."

"Scared?" queried Roger.

"Yes. When he saw me I thought he was going to run away. I asked him if he had seen anything, and when he answered me his face went almost white. I reckon he was scared—thinking of the way he treated you folks on the trail. Maybe he thought I was goin' to pitch into him for it."

"Maybe," said Dave, slowly. "He hadn't seen anything of the thieves?"

"No. He said he didn't know the hosses was gone until his father told him. He said he got lost in the woods, and stayed in a certain spot till the blow was over."

"Humph!" murmured Dave, and there the talk came to an

Edward Stratemeyer

end. But Dave was not satisfied. He still wondered if Link Merwell knew anything about the taking of the horses.

CHAPTER XX

FISHING AND HUNTING

The remainder of the week went by, and the boys and girls amused themselves as best they could. During that time, Mr. Endicott received a visit from the sheriff of the county, and Dave and his chums were called upon to tell all they could about the missing horses. Then, after some whispered talk between the county official and the ranch owner, the lads were requested to describe the man who had been seen on the trail in company with Link Merwell.

"I really think the fellow was Andy Andrews," said the sheriff. "But if so, he had a big nerve to show himself in these parts."

"Didn't you ask Link about the man?" asked Dave.

"Yes. He says the fellow was a stranger to him, and they were just riding together for company. He says they were together about half an hour before he met you on the trail, and that the fellow left him about a quarter of an hour later and headed in the direction of the railroad station. He said the fellow didn't give any name, but said he was looking up some ranch properties for some Chicago capitalists."

This was all the sheriff could tell, and on that the matter, for the time being, rested. Fortunately, Star Ranch possessed a good number of horses, so none of the young folks were deprived of mounts. But Belle mourned the loss of her favorite

Edward Stratemeyer

steed, to which she had become greatly attached.

"I don't care so much for the others, but I do hope papa gets back Lady Alice," she said, dolefully.

A spell of bad weather kept the young folks indoors for the time being, and one day they were reminded by a cowboy of the entertainment they had promised.

"As soon as it clears, we'll give you an exhibition of fancy ridin'," said the cowboy. "But jest now the boys are dyin' fer some good singin' an' music, and such."

Dave and the others got their heads together, and the upshot of the matter was that an entertainment was arranged, to be given in the big dining-hall of the ranch house. One end of this room was elevated to form a stage, with big portieres for curtains, and Roger, Phil, and Dave rehearsed several of the "turns" they had done at various times at Oak Hall. The girls practiced a number of songs, and Laura and the senator's son decided to give a dialogue, which they called "Which Mr. Brown Lives Here?"

Word was passed around about the coming entertainment, and it was announced that it would be for the benefit of an old lady, the mother of a cowboy who had been killed in a cattle stampede the season before. The tickets were placed at one dollar each, the entire proceeds to go to the old lady. This charity appealed to the cowboys, and every one on the place took a ticket, and then got the cowboys from neighboring ranches to do likewise.

"We'll have to let some of them sit on the veranda and look in through the windows," said Mrs. Endicott, when she heard how many tickets had been sold. "The room won't hold half of them."

"If we have to, we'll give a double performance," said Dave. "We want everybody to get his money's worth." And then it was arranged that tickets should be good for either the "matinee" or the night performance.

The first performance was given in the afternoon and lasted from three to half-past five o'clock. Every number on the programme went off without a hitch, and the cowboys applauded uproariously. During the intermission one cowboy got up very gravely and marched to the stage, where he deposited a round Indian basket.

"Fer extra contributions, boys!" he sang out, loudly. "Don't be tight when thar's an old lady to help!" And he dropped two silver dollars in the basket. At once the other cowboys sprang up and marched to the front, and a steady stream of silver poured into the basket, much to the delight of everybody.

"Financially, this is going to be a great success," said Dave, his face beaming. "I only hope they really like the show."

"They do, or they would soon let you know," answered Belle. "A cowboy isn't so polite as to make believe he likes a thing when he doesn't."

The evening crowd was even larger than that which had gathered in the afternoon, and the seating capacity of the dining-room and the veranda near the windows was taxed to its utmost. The boys and girls started in to give exactly the same show as during the afternoon, and the first part went off very well. The Indian basket was again brought into play, and once more a shower of silver was poured into it.

"Mrs. Chambers will be more than delighted," said Belle.

"How much money do you think we will have for her?" asked Jessie.

"Oh, ticket money and extra contributions, at least two hundred dollars. It will be a splendid aid to the old lady."

During the first part of the evening's entertainment, Dave had been much surprised to note the entrance of Hank Snogger, accompanied by two other cowboys from the Merwell ranch. Snogger looked a bit sheepish, as if realizing that he was out of his element. The other two cowboys were rough and hard-looking men, and had evidently been drinking.

"I didn't think we'd have anybody here from the Merwell place," whispered Phil.

"Well, I suppose some of our cowboys sold them the tickets," answered Dave. "I certainly didn't think that fellow, Snogger, would show himself."

"The men with him are pretty loud," said Roger. "I hope they don't try to break up the show."

The second half of the entertainment was in full swing when one of the men with Snogger commenced to laugh uproariously. His companion joined in, and both made such a noise that not a word spoken on the stage could be heard by the rest of the audience.

"Say, keep quiet there!" called out Sid Todd, who was acting as a sort of usher.

The two cowboys paid no attention to this request, but continued to laugh, and presently one of them joined in the chorus of one of the songs the girls and boys were rendering. He sang badly out of tune, and made such a discord that the song had to come to a stop.

"Go on! Go on!" he yelled, loudly.

"Whoop her up, everybody!" called his companion. "All join in the glad refrain!" And he started to sing in a heavy, liquor-laden voice.

"You shut up or git out!" cried Sid Todd, striding forward.

"They don't mean no harm," put in Hank Snogger, but he did not speak in positive tones.

"You keep out of this, Snogger," answered Todd, coldly. "Those men have got to behave themselves or git out. I said it, an' I mean it."

"That's right—put 'em out!" shouted several.

"Ain't we got a right to laff?" demanded one of the cowboys who were making the disturbance.

"Yes, but not so as to drown everything else," answered Sid Todd. "An' you can't sing."

"We come here fer some fun," said the other cowboy from the Merwell ranch. "An' we are going to have it. Whoop her up, everybody!" And he commenced to sing once more.

There were cries from all sides, and for a minute it looked as if the entertainment would end in a general row. But then Sid Todd gave a signal to some of the other Endicott hands, and in a twinkling the two boisterous cowboys were grabbed and hustled from the house. One tried to draw his pistol, but was given a blow in the face that all but sent him flat.

"You brought those fellows over here—you take 'em away—an' mighty quick, too," said Sid Todd to Hank Snogger. And he gave the other cowboy such a black look that Snogger sneaked out of the house in a hurry. Outside, the three men were surrounded by a dozen of the Endicott hands, and they were forced to mount their horses and ride away; and that was the last seen of them for the time being.

The interruption made Laura and Jessie so nervous that they could not sing any more, so the programme had to be changed. Dave thought of a funny monologue Shadow Hamilton had once given at Oak Hall, and he gave this, as far as he could remember it, and put in a few stories that were new. The youth worked hard, and the cowboys applauded him vigorously when he had finished, and soon the unpleasant incident was practically forgotten. When the show was over, the cowboys all said it was the finest thing they had ever seen outside of a city theater.

"Worth the money," said one old cowboy. "An' I'd go ag'in to-morrow night, ef I could." Entertainments in that locality were rare, and the show was a grand treat to all.

"Oh, but those men who laughed and sang were horrid!" said Laura. "And I was so afraid they would start to shoot, I didn't know how to control myself!"

"I believe they came over here on purpose to spoil the entertainment," said Phil.

"But why should they do that?" asked Jessie, innocently.

"More than likely Link Merwell got them to do it," answered Roger. "It would be of a piece with his meanness."

"I believe they were brought over by that Hank Snogger," said the shipowner's son.

"Yes, but I think Snogger is in some way under Link's thumb," put in Dave. "Anyway, the two seem to have a good deal in common."

"Well, it was a mean piece of business," said Belle. "Oh, I do wish the Merwells would sell out to some nice people! It would be splendid to have real good neighbors."

On the following Monday the boys went fishing "on their own hook," as Phil expressed it, although Jessie said he had better say "hooks," since they proposed to use several of them. The boys rode over to the river and took with them their shotguns. While fishing they kept their horses in sight and their firearms ready for use, and had any horse-thieves shown themselves they would have met with a hot reception. Fishing proved good, and inside of three hours they had all the fish on their strings that they cared to carry.

"Let us ride up the river a bit," suggested Phil, after they had eaten their lunch. "I'd like to look at the country, and it is possible we may be able to stir up some game."

As it was a clear day, the others agreed, and soon they were riding slowly along a trail which wound in and out among the rocks bordering the stream. They passed the shack which Roger and the girls had used as a shelter from the storm, and then reached an open spot. Beyond was a high hill, covered with a primeval forest.

"There ought to be some game in that woods," said Dave, as they continued to move forward.

"If the cowboys haven't shot everything worth shooting," answered the senator's son. "There used to be good hunting in Maine and in Upper New York State, but you have got to tramp a good many miles these days before you catch sight of anything worth while."

After a ride in the sun it was cool and pleasing in the forest, and they took their time riding under the great trees, some of which must have been fifty to a hundred years old. They saw a number of birds flitting about, but did not attempt to bring any down.

"If we want any big game we must keep quiet," said Dave, and after that they moved along without speaking, and with their eyes and ears on the alert for the first sign of something worth shooting.

Presently Dave held up his hand and all came to a halt. Not far away could be heard a curious drumming sound.

"What's that?" whispered Phil.

"Sounds like grouse," answered Dave. "They drum like that sometimes. They must be over in the trees yonder. Let us dismount and see."

The others were willing, and leaving their horses tied to the trees, the three boys crept forward to the spot from which the drumming proceeded. They came up abreast, and soon all caught sight of a number of grouse of the sharp-tailed variety, huddled in a little opening among the bushes.

"Get ready and fire when I give the word," whispered Dave, and a few seconds later all three of the chums blazed away simultaneously. There was a fluttering and more drumming, and several grouse thrashed the ground.

"Hurrah! we've got four!" cried Roger, rushing forward.

"And this one makes five!" said Phil, and dispatched one that was fluttering around. Then Dave killed a sixth, and by that time the rest of the game was out of sight.

CHAPTER XXI

A WILDCAT AMONG THE HORSES

The bringing down of the grouse filled the boys with satisfaction, and they inspected the game with much interest.

"They'll make fine eating," declared Roger.

"Let us see if we can't get some more," pleaded Phil. The "fever" of hunting had taken possession of him.

"We'll not find much in this neighborhood," said Dave. "But I am willing to go a little further," he added, seeing how disappointed the shipowner's son looked.

Placing the game over their shoulders, they reloaded their weapons and continued on through the forest, taking a trail that seemed to have been made by wild animals. Twice they had to cross a winding brook, and at the second fording-place Dave, who was in the rear, called a halt.

"What do you want?" questioned Roger, as he and Phil turned back.

"I want you to look at these hoofmarks," answered Dave, and he pointed up the stream a short distance.

All passed to the locality indicated, and each youth looked at the hoofmarks with interest. They were made by a number of horses, probably six or eight, and though the marks were washed a little, as if by rain, they could still be plainly seen.

"Do you think they were made by the horses that were stolen, Dave?" questioned Phil.

"I don't know what to think."

"The horse-thieves might easily have come this way," said the senator's son. "They would be more apt to go away from the ranch than towards it."

"Maybe they stopped here during the big blow," said Phil.

"I think you are right, for here are marks where the animals were tied to trees," went on Dave. "I wonder—well, I declare!"

Dave stopped short and picked up a bit of a leather halter lying on the ground. It was of curious Mexican design, having a light leather thong entwined in a dark one.

"I don't know that I have ever seen a halter like that before," mused Roger, as he took the bit of halter from Dave, and then passed it to Phil.

"I have," answered Dave.

"So have I!" cried the shipowner's son. "Link Merwell's horse had one on, the day we met on the trail!"

"Just what I was going to say," added Dave. "I noticed it particularly."

"Then this must belong to Link," came from the senator's son.

"Perhaps not," answered Dave, slowly. "There may be other such halters around. We'll have to give Link the benefit of the doubt, you know."

"See here!" burst out Phil. "You may think as you please, but I have always thought that Link had something to do with the taking of our horses."

"Do you think he would deliberately steal six horses, Phil?"

"Well, maybe not deliberately steal them, but—but—I think he took them, anyhow."

"He may have taken them intending to drive them to our ranch, and perhaps the horses got away from him in the storm," suggested Roger.

"That may be true—it would be just like one of Link's mean tricks," answered Dave.

"I think we ought to tax him with it," said Phil.

"He'd deny it point-blank if you did," returned the senator's son. "This bit of halter is no proof against him. No, you'd only get into hot water if you accused him without proofs."

"What Roger says is true," declared Dave. "We'll not say a word against Link, or accuse him, until we have some good proof that he is guilty."

Taking the bit of halter with them, the three chums continued on their way along the trail. They covered another quarter of a mile, but saw no game excepting some birds on which they did not care to waste powder and shot.

"We'll have to go back, I suppose," said Phil, with a sigh. "Gracious, I wish we'd see a bear, or something!"

"How would an elephant and a few lions do?" quizzed Roger, with a grin.

"Or a couple of man-eating tigers," suggested Dave.

"I don't care! You can make fun if you want to, but I came out to this ranch to have some hunting," said Phil, stubbornly. "I'm going to the mountains and get something worth while some day."

"So are we all going, Phil," answered Dave, quickly. "I want to bring down some big game just as much as you do."

"Sid Todd said he'd take us," said Roger. "We'll make him keep his word."

They took a look around the locality where they were standing, and then turned back to where they had left their horses. They were still some distance from the animals when they heard one of the steeds give a sudden snort of alarm. Looking through the trees, they saw Phil's horse leap and plunge, and then the others did likewise, as if trying to break from their halters.

"Something is wrong!" cried Dave. "Come on, before the horses break away!"

"Something has scared them," put in Roger. "Keep your guns ready for a shot. It may be a bear!"

"No such luck!" declared Phil. Nevertheless, he swung his shotgun into position for firing, and his chums did likewise.

As the boys entered the opening where the horses were tied, Dave caught sight of what was causing the disturbance. Out on the branch of a tree, directly over the animals, was a chunky and powerful looking wildcat, commonly called in that section of the country a bobcat. Its eyes were gleaming wickedly, its teeth were exposed, and it acted as if ready to leap at the throat of one of the horses.

"Look!" cried Dave, and then, as quickly as he could, he leveled his shotgun, took aim, and fired. The report of the firearm was followed by a blood-curdling cry from the wildcat, and down from the tree limb it tumbled, to roll over and over on the ground between the horses.

"Oh, what a savage beast!" gasped Phil, and for the instant he was so taken aback that he did not know what to do.

"He'll drive the horses crazy!" shouted Roger. "Oh, if I could only get a shot at him!"

What the senator's son said about the horses was true. The wildcat had been badly, but not mortally, wounded, and now it was rolling and twisting on the ground, sending the dirt and leaves flying in all directions. The steeds were in a panic, and leaped and plunged hither and thither, doing their best to break away.

"I should have waited until we all had the chance to shoot," said Dave. "If I can catch my horse—"

He got no further, for just then Roger, seeing a chance, rushed in between two of the steeds and pulled both triggers of his shotgun in quick succession. His aim was true, and, hit in the side, the wildcat rolled over and then started to crawl back into some bushes.

"He is going!" shouted Dave.

"I must have a shot!" put in Phil, recovering somewhat, and now he blazed away. When the smoke rolled off, the boys saw that the wildcat had disappeared.

"Where is he?"

"He went into yonder bushes!"

"Is he dead, do you think?"

"I don't know. Be careful, or he may leap out at us."

Such were some of the remarks made as the three boys reloaded, in the meantime keeping their eyes on the spot where the wildcat had last been seen. The horses were still plunging, but gradually they quieted down.

"I am going to see if the wildcat is really dead," said Dave, boldly. "Even if he's alive, I don't think there is much fight left in him."

"You be careful!" warned Phil. "A wounded beast is always extra savage. He may fly at your throat, and then it will be all up with you."

"I guess we plugged him pretty well," said Roger.

With great caution Dave approached the bushes into which the wildcat had disappeared, and rather gingerly his chums followed him. They could see a trail of blood, which led to the bottom of a hollow between some rocks. Here they beheld the wildcat, stretched out on its side.

"Dead as a stone!" announced Dave, after a brief examination.

"Are you sure?" questioned Phil. "He may be shamming— some wild beasts do, you know."

"No, he's dead,—you can see for yourself."

"What shall we do with him?" questioned Roger, after all were convinced that the wildcat was really dead. "He isn't good for much."

"We could keep the skin—or have him stuffed," suggested Phil.

"Let us take him back to the ranch—so that the folks can see we really killed him," said Dave. "Then we might have him stuffed and sent to Oak Hall, to put in the museum."

"Just the thing!" cried the senator's son. "That will please Doctor Clay, I am sure."

They dragged the wildcat out into the open, and laid it where the horses might see that it was dead. As soon as they were aware of this, the steeds quieted down completely, and the boys had no more trouble with them. Dave and Phil carried the grouse and the fish, and Roger slung the wildcat up behind his saddle, and then off they set for Star Ranch at a gallop.

"Here come the fishermen!" cried Laura, who was out in front of the ranch house. "I hope you had luck!"

"We did," answered Dave, gayly. "How is that?" and he held up a string of fish.

"Splendid, Dave!"

"And how is that?" he went on, holding up two of the grouse.

"I declare, some game, too! Why, you've had good luck, haven't you!"

"Let me see!" said Belle, as she appeared, followed by Jessie.

"And how is this?" asked Phil, showing his fish and the rest of the game.

"Oh, how grand!" murmured Belle.

"What is that Roger has?" questioned Jessie.

"A wildcat!" cried the senator's son, and, leaping down, he brought the dead beast into full view. All the girls shrieked, and Jessie started to run back into the house. Hearing the commotion, Mrs. Endicott appeared, and then her husband.

"A bobcat!" cried the railroad president. "I didn't know there were any near this place. A big fellow, too," he added, as he inspected the animal.

"Did you shoot him, Roger?" asked Laura.

"We all had a hand in it," answered the senator's son. "Dave gave him the first dose of shot, and then Phil and I got in our work. It was a hard job to kill him, I can tell you," and then Roger told of how the wounded beast had fallen down among the horses.

"You can be thankful your horses didn't get away," said Mr. Endicott. "I knew of a horse once that was scared by a bear and he ran several miles, and wasn't caught until the next day."

"Oh, Dave, weren't you scared when you saw him on the tree?" whispered Jessie. She felt proud to think her hero had been the first to shoot at the beast.

"I didn't give myself time to get scared," he answered. "I just fired as quickly as I could."

"But supposing the wildcat had jumped on you!" And the girl shivered and caught him by the arm.

"I should have defended myself as best I could, Jessie."

"You—you mustn't take such risks," the pretty girl whispered, and looked wistfully into Dave's eyes. "I—I can't stand it, Dave!" And then she blushed and turned her face away.

"I'll be very careful after this, Jessie—for your sake," he answered, softly and tenderly.

CHAPTER XXII

COWBOY TRICKS AND "BRONCO-BUSTING"

"You boys sure did have a day of sport," said Sid Todd, after he had inspected the fish, the grouse, and the wildcat. "And you've proved that you can shoot," he added, nodding toward the slain beast. "I've known many a putty good hunter to get the shakes when he see a bobcat a-glarin' at him from a tree. It ain't no tender sight, is it now?"

"Not much!" answered Phil, warmly. He had been as close to getting the "shakes" as any one of the three. "I was glad when I knew he was dead."

"Something about a bobcat I don't like," went on the cowboy. "We used to hunt 'em—when they got after the sheep some years ago. Once one of 'em jest about got me by the throat, an' I ain't forgitting it! I'd rather face a bear, I think."

"You mustn't forget that you are to take us to the mountains on a hunting expedition," came from Roger. "We want to get some deer, or an elk, before we go back East."

"I'll take you—don't worry," answered the cowboy.

The news soon spread around the ranch that the "tenderfeet" had killed a big bobcat, and all the hands came to get a look at the beast. They praised the boys, and said they must be nervy hunters or they could not have done it. Of course the lads were

Edward Stratemeyer

correspondingly proud, and who can blame them? The animal was prepared for stuffing, and then sent off by express to a taxidermist in the city.

After talking the matter over among themselves, the boys decided to tell Mr. Endicott about the piece of Mexican halter they had picked up. He listened gravely to what they had to say, and looked at the bit of leather curiously.

"I am afraid it is not much in the way of evidence," said he. "But I'll remember it, and we'll have to watch Link Merwell—that is, as well as we can. There would be no gain in speaking to Mr. Merwell, it would only stir up the bad feeling that already exists. I understand that he has had an offer for his ranch from somebody in the East, and I trust he sells out and moves somewhere else."

"So do I," echoed Dave, heartily. "Some place where none of us will ever hear of him or his son again."

Two days after the shooting of the wildcat, Sid Todd announced that the cowboys of Star Ranch and Hooper Ranch, up the river, were going to hold a contest in "bronco-busting" and in fancy riding. All the young folks were invited to be present and a little stand was to be erected, from which they might view what was going on in comfort.

"Hurrah! that suits me!" cried Dave. "I've been wanting to see them break in a real bronco."

"And I want to see some of their fancy riding," added the senator's son. "It will be a real Wild West show."

"And no fifty cents admission, either," said Phil, with a grin.

"I hope nobody gets hurt," said Jessie, timidly.

"Oh, they are generally more careful than you think," answered Mr. Endicott.

"But bronco-busting is dangerous, isn't it?" questioned Laura.

"Yes,—for anybody who has had no experience. But Todd and some of the others can saddle and ride any pony in these parts."

All went out to the stretch of plain where the contest was to take place. The little stand was there, true enough, and to the four corners were nailed four flags—two of the Stars and Stripes, and one each of the two ranches, that of the Endicotts having a blue field with the words, Star Ranch, in white.

The word had been passed around for a good many miles, and consequently a crowd numbering over a hundred had assembled on the field, including half a dozen ladies and several children. The cowboys were out "on parade," as Mr. Endicott expressed it, and each wore his best riding outfit, and had his horse and trappings "slicked up" to the last degree. All wore their largest Mexican sombreros, and, taken together, they formed a truly picturesque assemblage.

"Puts me in mind of gypsies," said Laura. "Only they haven't their wives and children with them."

"And they aren't telling fortunes," added Jessie.

The sport began with some fancy riding in which eight of the cowboys, four from each ranch, participated. The cowboys would ride like the wind and leap off and on their steeds, turn from frontwards to backwards, slide from the saddle under their horses' necks and up into the saddle again, and lean low to catch up handkerchiefs and hats left on the grass for that purpose. Then they did some fancy vaulting, over bars and brushwood, and while riding two and even four horses.

"Good! good!" shouted Dave. "Isn't that fine!"

"Best I ever saw!" answered Roger, and everybody in the crowd applauded vigorously.

Edward Stratemeyer

After the fancy riding came some shooting while in the saddle, both at stationary objects and at things sprung into the air from a trap. The repeated crack! crack! crack! of the pistols and rifles scared some of the girls a little, but the boys enjoyed the spectacle thoroughly, and marveled at some of the shots made.

"Game wouldn't stand much chance with those chaps," remarked Dave. "They could hit a running deer or a flying bird without half trying."

The shooting at an end, the cowboys brought out their best lassoes and showed what could be done in landing the circlets over running steers and horses. Here Sid Todd was in his element, and the way he managed his lasso, one of extra length at that, brought out tremendous applause.

"He is the best lasso-thrower in these parts," said Mr. Endicott. "No one can compare with him."

"Well, he is a good shot, too," said Dave. "And he rides well also."

"Yes, he is a good all-around fellow," answered the ranch owner. "I am mighty glad I have him,—and I am glad I got rid of that Hank Snogger," he added.

"Are any of the men from the Merwell ranch here?"

"No, I warned them to keep away—after that trouble we had at your entertainment,—and Mr. Hooper, the owner of the other ranch,—told them to keep away, too. Some of those fellows drink, and if they got to quarreling there might be some shooting, and then there would be no telling where the thing would end. I made up my mind I'd take no chances."

The "bronco-busting," as it is called, was reserved for after lunch. Several wild-looking ponies were tethered at a distance, and it was the task of those who proposed to do the "busting" to take a saddle, fasten it on a pony, and then get up and ride around the field at least twice. The ponies were unbroken, and of the sort usually designated as vicious and unreliable.

It was truly a thrilling exhibition and one the boys, and the girls, too, for the matter of that, never forgot. As soon as a bronco was approached he would begin to plunge and kick, and to get a saddle on him was all but impossible. Then, if at last he was saddled, and the cowboy who had been successful got in the seat, the pony would leap and plunge some more, sometimes going straight up into the air and coming down with legs as stiff as posts. Then, if this did not throw the cowboy off, the pony would start to run, only to stop short suddenly, in the hope of sending the rider over his head.

"Oh, somebody will be killed!" screamed Jessie, and often turned her face away to shut out the sight. "Oh, why do they do such dreadful things?" she added.

"They've got to break the ponies somehow," answered Dave. "Those broncos will be all right after they get used to it."

"Say, do you know, I'd like to try that," remarked Roger. "I think I could sit on one of those ponies, if he had the saddle on."

"I think I could do it, too," added Dave.

"Oh, Dave!" exclaimed his sister, while Jessie gave a little shriek of horror.

"It's not as bad as it looks—after the pony is saddled," answered Dave.

"We'll try it to-morrow—on the quiet," whispered Roger.

After the "busting" of the broncos had come to an end, there was a two-mile race, for a first and a second prize, put up by the two ranch owners. In this race nine of the cowboys started, amid a wild yelling and the cracking of numerous pistols,—for the average cowboy is not enjoying himself unless he can make a noise.

"They are off!" yelled Phil.

"Yes, and see them go!" added Dave.

"I'll bet our ranch wins!" came from Roger.

"What will you bet?" asked Belle, mischievously.

"A box of candy against a cream pie."

"That's fair,—but I can't bet against our ranch," answered Belle, gayly.

On and on thundered the horses across the plains, to a spot a mile distant. At first three of the cowboys from the other ranch were in the lead, and their followers cheered them loudly.

"Oh, we are going to lose!" said Belle, with a pout, as the leaders in the race started on the return.

"No! no!" answered Dave. "See, Sid Todd is coming to the front."

"Yes, and Yates is crawling up, too," added Phil.

Nearer and nearer to the finish line swept the cowboys, those in the rear doing their best to forge ahead. Now Sid Todd, Yates, and two cowboys from the Hooper ranch were neck-and-neck.

"It will be a tie," murmured Laura.

"No, Todd is gaining!" cried Mr. Endicott, who was as much excited as anybody. "See, he and Hooper's man are now ahead!"

"Here they come, on the homestretch!" was the general cry.

On and on thundered the horses, nearer and nearer to the finishing line. When the leaders were less than fifty yards off Sid Todd made a spurt.

"Here comes Todd!"

"Todd wins! Todd wins!"

"Galpey is second!"

"Yes, and Yates is third!"

"Say, that's riding for you!" And so the cries rang out. Sid Todd had indeed won, and all of his friends from Star Ranch congratulated him. The second prize went to the cowboy from the Hooper ranch. Yates got nothing, but was content to know that he had come in third and only five yards behind the leader.

"Well, that certainly was an entertainment worth looking at," said Dave, when it was over, and they were returning to the ranch house.

"I've never been so stirred up," answered Roger. "But, say, I am going to try one of those broncos to-morrow," he added.

"Not for me!" said Phil. "I value my neck too much."

"What about you, Dave?" And the senator's son looked anxiously at the Crumville lad.

"Well, I'll see," answered Dave. He was not afraid to try riding a bronco, but he did not wish to worry Jessie and his sister.

"You are not afraid, are you?"

"No."

"Well, I am not afraid, either," came quickly from Phil, and his face grew red. "You needn't think—"

"Oh, don't get mad, Phil; I didn't mean anything," interposed Roger. "If you don't care to try it, you don't have to."

"But you needn't insinuate that I—"

"I am not insinuating anything, Phil. I merely wanted to know if Dave will try riding with me, that's all."

"Well, I—er—I know what you think. And if you try this bronco-busting business, why—I'll try it too, so there!" answered Phil, defiantly.

At the house the talk was entirely of the things they had seen. Jessie was rather glad it was over, for rough things made her somewhat afraid. Belle was enthusiastic and said she had once tried "bronco-busting" herself.

"But I didn't do much," she said. "The pony started to run and then stopped suddenly, and I went over his head into a stack of hay. I was glad the hay was there, otherwise I might have broken some of my bones."

"It is dangerous sport at the best," said Mrs. Endicott. "But the cowboys feel that the ponies must be broken in, and there is no other way to do it."

CHAPTER XXIII

DAVE ON A BRONCO

Dave had his doubts about doing any "bronco-busting" on his own account, but he did not say anything to Roger and Phil about it. He was not afraid, but he knew Jessie would be greatly worried if he attempted anything dangerous.

However, his chums got him up early the following morning, and, directly after breakfast, Roger led the way down to the corral.

"I am going to try it, even if you are not," said the senator's son, and insisted upon it that one of the unbroken ponies be brought forward. The saddle was adjusted by Sid Todd, who held the animal while Roger leaped into the saddle.

The experience was not as exciting as had been anticipated, for the reason that the animal chosen by Todd was somewhat tame. The cowboy was attached to the boys, and did not wish to see any of them run the risk of breaking his neck.

After Roger came Phil, and he was timid enough to ask for a horse "that didn't look as if he wanted to eat somebody up." Phil had more of a time of it than Roger, but managed to keep in the saddle and ride around the corral several times.

"It's not so hard as I supposed," said the shipowner's son, as he leaped to the ground, and the pony, freed of the saddle, galloped off. "I thought I'd be half-killed."

"Those ponies were not so wild as those used yesterday," answered Dave. "Not but that they were bad enough," he continued, with a smile.

Sid Todd had remained to hold the pony ridden by Phil and had then been called away to attend to some business at another part of the ranch. He had told Yates to help the boys.

Now, as it happened, Yates was full of fun and always up to practical jokes. It had disgusted him to see Todd bring out such comparatively safe ponies as those ridden by Roger and Phil. He had been told to bring out a certain animal for Dave, but instead led forth a bronco that was as wild and fiery as any used the day previous.

"If he rides that beast, he's a good one," Yates murmured to himself, and then he beckoned to some other cowboys to watch the fun. Half a dozen quit work to draw closer, each with a broad grin on his sunburnt face. They expected to see Dave get the shaking-up of his life and felt positive he would not be able to stay on the bronco's back two minutes.

"He certainly is a wild one," said Dave, as he advanced and eyed the pony.

"Oh, he's no worse than the others," answered Yates, smoothly, and then he rolled his eyes and winked at the other cowboys.

Dave looked critically at the saddle and saw to it that it was properly buckled. Then he flung his cap to Roger.

"Say, Dave, that pony looks half-crazy," said Phil. "You be careful."

"He certainly does look wild," added Roger.

"Well, I'm going to ride him anyway—or know the reason why!" cried Dave, and a look of strong determination came into his face. "Get around there!" he called sharply to the pony, and then, with a quick leap, he gained the saddle and dug his knees into the pony's sides. "Let him go!"

Yates released his hold and everybody in the crowd backed away. For a moment the bronco stood stock-still, his eyes gazing straight ahead. Then he gave a vigorous shake and took a few steps forward.

"Hurrah! see him ride!" shouted Yates, and winked again at the other cowboys, who grinned more than ever.

Five steps forward and the bronco halted. Then up in the air he went, a distance of six or eight feet. He came down "on all fours," good and hard, and had Dave been resting in the saddle he would have had the wind knocked out of him completely. But the youth was standing in the stirrups, and he allowed his body to spring with that of the animal he hoped to conquer.

Three times the bronco tried this trick, and the third time Dave came close to falling off. Then the bronco gave a dart forward, like an arrow from a bow.

"There he goes!" yelled the senator's son, but the words were not yet out of his mouth when the bronco stopped short. Dave slid to the animal's neck, but there he clung, his face pale and determined, and his teeth set.

"Hi! hi! what's this!" shouted a voice, and, turning, the crowd saw Sid Todd approaching on the run. "Yates, what do you mean by letting him git up on that critter?" he demanded, indignantly.

"Ain't that the bronco you wanted him to try?" asked the other cowboy, innocently.

"No—an' you know it!" stormed Todd. "Do you want him to

break his neck? Hi, Dave, jump down! You can't tame that beast, nohow!"

"I—I'm all—ri—right!" jerked out Dave, between his teeth. "Ke—keep away," he added, as Todd came closer, to lend his assistance.

"He's a bad one, boy—one o' the worst on the ranch. Yates had no call to offer him to you."

"Ke—keep away," was all Dave replied. He could not say more, for the bronco claimed all his attention.

"Yates, if that boy is hurt, you'll have an account to settle with me," said Sid Todd, and shook his fist at the other cowboy.

"I—er—I was sure you wanted me to bring out that beast fer him," murmured Yates, uneasily. He was sorry now that he had played the trick on Dave.

The bronco had taken another run, coming to as sudden a halt as before. Dave slid up almost to the animal's ears, but still clung on, and quickly regained his seat in the saddle. Then, without warning, the pony dropped to the ground and started to roll over.

"Look out! you'll have your leg broken!" yelled Phil. But Dave was on his guard, and, as the pony dropped, he leaped away to safety. Then, as the animal arose once more, the youth grabbed the saddle and vaulted into the seat.

"Say, that's goin' some, I tell you!" roared one of the cowboys in delight. "He ain't givin' in yet, he ain't!"

"Look out that he don't bang you into a fence, or one of the buildings!" yelled Sid Todd. He was alarmed, yet delighted at the manner in which Dave clung to his difficult and dangerous undertaking.

With Dave once more on his back, the pony tried new tactics. Around and around he went in a circle, sending the dust of the corral flying in all directions. Then, like lightning, he reversed, nearly breaking his own neck, and causing Dave to slip far down on the outer side. But the youth hung to the saddle, and, leaning forward, slapped the bronco a smart crack on the neck. This he followed up with a blow on the head.

The effect was just what the boy desired. The pony forgot all his tricks, and leaping high into the air, he shot off like a streak toward the corral gate. Once outside, he headed for the open plains, going with the speed of a racer on the track.

"They're off!" cried Roger.

"Don't let him throw you!" yelled Todd.

"Can't we ride after 'em?" queried Phil.

"Sure we can ride after 'em," responded Todd. "An' we better do it, too, fer there ain't no tellin' what that pony will do to Dave," he added, anxiously, and with a black look at Yates, which made the other cowboy cast his eyes to the ground.

On and on sped the bronco, with Dave sitting firmly in the saddle. So long as the pony kept going, the lad felt he had nothing to fear. But he was on the alert, for he did not know but that the animal would play another trick at any instant.

"Go on, old boy!" he muttered. "We've got miles and miles of prairie ahead of us. Run till you are tired! But remember, you've got to carry me back," he added, grimly.

Soon the ranch house and the corral were mere specks in the distance, and then even these faded from view. The pony kept to the open country, and not once did he slacken his speed.

"I guess he'll drop into a walk when his wind is gone," thought Dave. But the pony's breathing apparatus showed no sign of giving out. Dave allowed his eyes to turn back, and calculated he had gone two or three miles. "Maybe we had better turn back now," he murmured, and tried to guide the steed in a circle. But this was a failure. The pony kept straight ahead, running due eastward, as the youth could see by the sun.

"All right, go as far as you please," said Dave, grimly. "If you can stand it, so can I," and he settled in the saddle.

Another two miles were covered, and then the bronco commenced to slacken his speed. Dave was on guard at this, and it was well to be, for, a second later, the pony once more tried the trick of flinging his rider over his head. But the effort was a failure, and in return Dave dug his knees deeply into the steed's ribs. Then off went the pony on a run again.

This time the bronco did not cover over a mile before dropping into a walk. Then Dave tried again to turn the animal, but without success.

"Don't want to go back, eh?" said the youth. "Well, you've got to, and that is all there is to it!" And he hit the pony a sharp slap on the neck and dug his knees into the animal's ribs as before.

The bronco was now losing courage. He commenced to run, but did not keep it up for more than a hundred yards. But when he dropped into a walk, Dave urged him up, and again he ran, but now only a dozen steps. Then the youth pulled on the left rein, and the bronco came around with scarcely any trouble.

"You aren't mastered yet, but you're pretty close to it," said the boy. "We are going home, understand, home!"

The bronco moved forward about a hundred feet. Then he deliberately dropped on the prairie and lay on his side, as quiet as a lamb.

"Want to rest, eh?" said Dave. "Well, not out here. You brought me here and you've got to take me back. Get up!"

He gave the animal a prod in the side. The bronco kicked out. Then Dave gave a harder prod. This the pony would not stand, and up he came with surprising agility. He tried to bolt, but Dave caught the saddle and clung there. They headed again eastward, away from the ranch.

"All right, now run for it, and keep it up as long as you please!" cried the boy, and urged the steed forward. Over the prairie the pony sped, as if he had just started in the race. Thus another mile was covered, and now Dave calculated he must be six or seven miles from Star Ranch. The country about him looked strange, and he wondered where he was. Nothing in the shape of a trail had come to view during the last run.

When the bronco stopped his racing, the youth turned him around again. He now showed signs of fatigue, but Dave urged him on, digging his knees into the animal's ribs as tightly as ever. Dave was almost "used up" himself, but he resolved to make the bronco take him back to the corral or die in the attempt.

"They shan't have the laugh on me," he argued. "It's back to the ranch or nothing!"

Dave steered the best course he could for the corral, but with nothing to guide him he did not know if he was moving exactly in the right direction or not. He kept on, with his eyes trying to look beyond the wide-stretching prairies.

Presently he saw in the distance what looked to be a row of low buildings. He headed in that direction, and then saw that the objects were moving towards him.

"They can't be buildings, for buildings don't move like that," he mused. "Must be cattle, or horses. Cattle, most likely."

Edward Stratemeyer

To avoid the cattle, he turned slightly southward. But the animals kept coming closer, and now he saw that they were running in something of a semicircle.

"Can anything be wrong with them?" he asked himself, and watched the approaching herd with interest. The bronco, too, pricked up his ears, and gave a sudden snort of alarm.

Then to Dave's ears came the thunder of the herd's hoofs, and he saw that the cattle were on a mad run. He drew rein and stood up in his stirrups.

The sight that met his gaze was truly alarming. At least a thousand head of steers were coming toward him, running swiftly, and with their horns bent low.

"They have stampeded!" he gasped. "And they are coming straight this way! What shall I do to escape them?"

CHAPTER XXIV

THE CATTLE STAMPEDE

Dave had often heard of cattle stampedes, and he knew how truly dangerous such a mad rush can become. Sometimes, from practically no cause whatever, a herd of cattle will start on a wild run, going they know not where, and carrying all down before them.

What had started the present stampede did not interest the youth, but he was interested in the question of how he might get out of the herd's way, so that he would not be run down and trodden to a jelly. To scare the leaders off might be easy, but would not those in the rear push on until he was simply overwhelmed?

"I've got to get away somehow!" he reasoned, and turned his pony at right angles to the approaching cattle. For the moment the bronco seemed too frightened to budge, but at a cry from Dave, he leaped forward, and then went streaking across the prairies as if he knew his life and that of his rider depended on his speed.

It was now a race for life, for the cattle were still moving in something of a semicircle, and Dave did not know whether or not he would be able to clear the end of the line before it reached him. He called to the pony, but this was unnecessary, for the bronco evidently understood the peril fully as well as his rider.

Edward Stratemeyer

Suddenly, when it looked as if pony and youth could not escape, Dave heard a whistle float across the prairie. Looking in the direction, he made out the form of Sid Todd, riding like the wind toward him. Behind him came Roger and Phil, but the two boys were soon stopped and told to go back.

"I'll head 'em off!" yelled Todd, coming closer. And waving his big sombrero in one hand he commenced to fire his pistol with the other. He shot rapidly, aiming for the ground and sending streaks of dust into the air. All the time he yelled at the top of his lungs, and, understanding the move, Dave yelled too, and swung one arm wildly.

Soon the leaders of the herd took notice and came to a sudden halt. The rest of the cattle shoved from behind, and then the leaders broke, some going to the right, and the others to the left.

"Look out, Roger! Phil! They are coming your way!" screamed Dave.

He was right, and for the minute it looked as if Dave had been saved at the expense of his chums. But only a few cattle were headed for the other boys, and as soon as Roger and Phil commenced to yell and wave their arms, these broke again, and thus the herd was completely scattered. They ran a short distance further, then halted, and a little later began to graze as if nothing out of the ordinary had happened.

"Are you all right, son?" asked Sid Todd, anxiously, as he ranged up beside Dave.

"Yes, but—I—I am a lit—tle wi—winded," answered Dave, when he could speak.

"Good enough! Then you mastered the bronco, eh? Didn't he throw you at all?"

"No."

"Didn't he roll?"

"Oh, yes, and I got off and on pretty quick, I can tell you."

"It's wonderful! I never would have thought it!" And Sid Todd's face showed his great admiration. "Why, don't you know that that is one of the wickedest ponies on this ranch? Yates and some of the others have tried to ride him more than once."

"And they couldn't do it?"

"Not much they couldn't! Why, that pony bit one of the men in the arm when he got too near!"

"He snapped at me once."

"Did, eh?"

"Yes, and I slapped his face."

"Well, that's the best way—show 'em you ain't afraid. But it's wonderful! When I see you on this pony I was sure you'd be killed, and I made up my mind to give Yates the wust lickin' he ever had."

"He's as mild as a lamb now," went on Dave, as he eyed the pony.

"Don't you go for to trustin' him too much, yet," were Sid Todd's words of warning, and Dave took them to heart, and it was well he did so, for while returning to the ranch, the bronco tried several tricks to get rid of his rider, but without success.

"I never thought you would do it," said Roger, earnestly. "Are you sure he is safe now?" he added, anxiously.

"I wouldn't try to ride that beast for a million dollars," was Phil's comment. "When he went off with you I thought you'd never get back to tell the story. Roger and I and Todd were so worried we rode after you just as fast as we could."

"I hope the girls don't hear of this," said Dave. "If they do, they'll worry themselves sick every time we go out."

"Oh, we've got to let folks know how you busted that bronco!" cried Sid Todd. "Why, son, you don't understand, but it's the finest bit o' bustin' ever done on this ranch!" he added, vehemently.

"Well, I am glad I won out, for one thing," answered Dave, dryly. "You won't have to give Yates that licking." And this remark made the cowboy laugh in spite of himself. Nevertheless, later on he gave Yates a lecture that the latter never forgot.

"The boy had one chanct in a hundred o' winning out," was what he said. "One chanct in a hundred, an' you knew it! If he had broken his neck I'd 'a' held you responsible, an' so would the boss."

"But he's a great rider," pleaded Yates.

"Sure he is, better nor you'll be if you live to be a hundred, Yates. But it was wrong to pile such a thing up his back,—an' don't you go for to do it again."

The news soon spread that Dave had "busted" the wild bronco, and this, coupled with the fact that he had aided in bringing down the bobcat, gave him an enviable reputation among the cowboys. But the girls were quite alarmed, Jessie and Laura especially.

"Oh, Dave, how could you!" cried Jessie, when they were alone.

"Well, Jessie, you wouldn't want me to appear like a coward, would you?" he asked.

"No, of course not, Dave! But—if you had been—killed!"

"I was watching out, I can tell you that," he answered, and then changed the subject, for he did not like to see the girl he admired so distressed.

After the excitement of the bronco riding, the boys were glad enough to take it easy for several days. Belle had a tennis court and a croquet ground, and they played each game for hours at a time. The girls were all good players and won the majority of the games.

"Tennis and croquet are all well enough when you have nice girls to play with," remarked Roger. "But otherwise I fancy I'd find them dead slow."

"He'd play twenty-four hours at a stretch with Laura," was Phil's comment.

"Not to mention how long you'd play with Belle," retorted the senator's son.

"Dave doesn't care to play at all when Jessie is around," went on Phil, slyly.

"Neither of 'em cares to play—if there's a hammock and a chair handy," added Roger.

"I noticed yesterday, when Jessie and I were playing tennis, you fellows were so busy talking to the girls you forgot all about your games," retorted Dave. "And one of you was spouting poetry, about 'eyes divine,' or something like that."

"Not me!" cried Roger.

"Then it must have been Phil!"

"No, it was Roger," protested the shipowner's son. "I saw him writing poetry when he should have been sending a letter home."

"You go on, you manufacturer of bombastic fairy tales!" cried the senator's son, and he commenced to chase Phil around the piazza. The other boy leaped the rail and Roger followed, and then both commenced to wrestle on the grass.

"Mercy me! What's going on?" cried Laura, coming from the sitting-room.

"Greatest exhibition on the globe!" called out Dave, in showman style. "The two marvelous lightweights of the United States, Master Hitem Morr and Lamem Lawrence. They will fight to a finish, without gloves, weather permitting. Walk up, tumble up, or crawl up! Admission ten cents, one dime; young ladies with grandfathers in arms, half-price!"

"Oh, Dave!" cried his sister, and burst out laughing. The noise brought Jessie and Belle to the scene, and seeing what was going on, all of the girls commenced to pelt the boys on the grass with tennis balls. The "attack" lasted for several minutes, and then the girls ran away, and the boys went after them, into the house and out again, and across the yard, and then through the kitchen, much to the astonishment of the Chinese cook. Here Phil scooped up a ladleful of soup.

"Halt, base enemy!" he cried, holding the soup aloft. "One step closer and thou shalt be—" And then he slipped and the soup slopped over his hand and his shoes. He ran for the yard again, dropped on a bench, in mock exhaustion; and there the others joined him; and the fun, for the time being, came to an end.

"We are going to the railroad station this afternoon with papa," said Belle. "Want to go along?"

"Will a duck drink ice-cream soda!" cried Roger. "Of course we will go along."

"Then you had better get ready now—for we are to start directly after lunch."

"Anything special at the station?" questioned Dave.

"Papa is going to see a man about some horses. He wants to buy a few more good ones, if he can."

"It's a pity we can't find out what became of the others," went on Dave.

It took the girls some time to prepare for the journey to the railroad station, so the start from Star Ranch was not made until after two o'clock. Mr. Endicott rode in advance, and the young folks paired off in couples after him.

When they got to the bridge Dave was much surprised to see a couple of men at work repairing the structure. They were putting down some planking that was bound to last a long while.

"Mr. Merwell must have opened his heart at last," said Dave, to the railroad president.

"Not at all, Dave; I am having this work done," was Mr. Endicott's reply.

"But I thought you said it was up to Mr. Merwell to keep this bridge in repair."

"So it is, but as he won't do anything, rather than have a quarrel, I am repairing it myself."

"Do you think he wants to sell out? Maybe that is his reason for not spending money in repairs."

"He will sell out, but his price is very high—too high to suit the man who wants to buy."

Leaving the vicinity of the bridge, the party continued on the way to the railroad station. The train was not yet in, but it soon arrived and on it came the man Mr. Endicott wished to see. From the train also stepped Hank Snogger. The ranch hand had evidently been to a barber in the city, for he was shaven and his hair was closely trimmed.

"He looks like quite a different person," remarked Belle. "He always wore his hair long and straggly before."

"Yes, and he wasn't any too clean," answered Dave. "Now he is well washed and brushed."

Hank Snogger walked around the station on an errand, and then came up to where a horse was waiting for him. As he did this he passed quite close to the boys and girls and gave the former a cold stare.

"Do you know, I feel sure I have seen somebody that looks like him," said Dave in a whisper. "I said so before. But I can't place the man."

"Yes, I've seen somebody that looked like him, too," added Roger. "It was while we were coming out here. Now let me think." And he rubbed his chin reflectively.

"Here's a letter about that boy we helped, Charley Gamp," said Phil, who had just received the mail.

"Charley Gamp!" cried Dave. "That's it—that's the same face! This Hank Snogger looks exactly like Charley Gamp!"

CHAPTER XXV

THE BEGINNING OF THE GRAND HUNT

Dave's announcement produced a little sensation, and for the moment his chums stared at him in astonishment.

"Come to think of it, that man does look like the little news-boy," said Roger, slowly. "Do you suppose they can be related?"

"I'd hate to think that Charley Gamp was related to such a fellow," said Phil. "Snogger isn't a nice sort to have anything to do with."

"Mr. Endicott said he didn't use to be so bad," answered Dave. "It is only lately—since he went to work for Mr. Merwell— that he has grown dissolute."

"Maybe he is sorry that he left the Endicott place," said the senator's son. "I'll wager he has no such nice times at the Triple X Ranch as he had at the Star."

"Not if all the cowboys are like those who came to our entertainment," said Phil. "But, Dave, if you think he's related to Charley Gamp, why not speak to him about it?"

"You may get into trouble if you do," interposed Roger, hastily. "Some of these Western characters don't like to have their past raked up."

"But Charley Gamp wants to find his relatives," went on the shipowner's son.

"I'll bring it around—when I get the chance," said Dave. "But I can't do it now," he added. "He's gone." And Dave was right. Hank Snogger had leaped on his horse, and was off, on a trail that led up the river instead of across it.

"What are you boys confabbing about?" cried Belle, coming up, with a box of candy in her hand.

"We were just wondering where we'd get some candy," answered Dave, innocently. He did not think it wise to mention Snogger just then.

"Indeed! Well, I bought this from the candy man of the train. He is waiting for the down train."

"Where is he?" questioned Roger.

"Down the track—by the water tower."

"We'll raid him!" cried the senator's son, and then he and Dave and Phil set off on a footrace in the direction of the man who sold candy, cigars, and magazines. They found that he had a pretty fair stock of candy and magazines, and each boy purchased what he thought would suit the others and himself. In the fun and good spirits that followed Hank Snogger was, for the time being, forgotten.

Two days later there was a rounding-up of some of the cattle and the boys were allowed to participate. They went out with Sid Todd, who had charge of the round-up, and were in the saddle from early morning until late at night. The cattle were gathered in a valley up the river, sorted out from some belonging to Mr. Merwell and Mr. Hooper, and then driven off to a stockyard along the railroad line.

"Not so exciting as I thought it would be," said Dave, after the round-up was over.

"I've had all the riding I want for one day," answered the shipowner's son.

"That's right," grumbled Roger. They had had only a quarter of an hour's rest for lunch. "I reckon some of us will be stiff in the morning," and he was right, all felt somewhat sore.

The round-up had been a careful one, for Mr. Endicott had heard that Mr. Merwell was finding fault over the way some of his cattle were being chased by the cowboys. The following afternoon the Merwells—father and son—met Mr. Endicott as he and Belle were riding along the trail, talking over the family's plans for the coming winter.

"See here, I want to speak about my cattle," cried Mr. Merwell, wrathfully, as he drew rein.

"Some time when I am alone, Mr. Merwell," answered the railroad president. He quickly saw that his neighbor was "spoiling for a fight."

"Your men took three or four of my steers," went on Mr. Merwell. "I won't stand for it."

"That can't be so, Mr. Merwell. My man, Todd, is a careful rounder, and he told me he was sure of the brands."

"He ain't careful at all," broke in Link. "He drinks and he don't know what he is doing."

"This is an affair between your father and myself," said Mr. Endicott, stiffly. "You will kindly keep out of it."

"Huh! I guess I can have my say!" growled Link.

"I shall hold you responsible for every head of cattle of mine that is missing," continued Mr. Merwell, with a dark look.

Edward Stratemeyer

"I am willing to pay for every head that Todd drove off that did not belong to us," answered Mr. Endicott. "But he assured me that he took only our own. I will look into the matter when I get back to the ranch." And, bowing stiffly, the railroad president rode on, with Belle beside him. As they passed, Link "made a face" at Belle, but the young lady refused to notice him.

As soon as he returned to the ranch, Mr. Endicott called up Sid Todd, and then some of the other cowboys, and questioned them closely about the cattle sent off. The head herder indignantly denied that he had included any outside cattle, and his story was corroborated by the others.

"I can leave it to Bill Parker, Mr. Hooper's man," said Todd. "He was there. If Merwell didn't want to take our word, why didn't he send a man down? We notified him that we was going to make a shipment."

"Have the steers been shipped yet?"

"No—not till to-morrow."

"Then ride down to the yard and have Harrison go over them and write out a declaration that they are all ours," added the ranch owner.

"It's a good deal of work," grumbled the cowboy.

"I know it, but I'll pay Harrison. With a declaration from Harrison, Mr. Merwell will have no claim."

The ranch owner's orders were carried out, and the next day a duplicate of the stockyard man's declaration,—that the cattle were all of the Star Ranch brand,—was delivered to Mr. Merwell.

"Huh! needn't tell me!" he sniffed, after reading the paper. "I guess Harrison is playing into Endicott's hands."

"You tell Harrison that—if you dare," answered the messenger, who had delivered the paper. Harrison was known to be a fair and square but high-tempered individual, and one who could shoot, and shoot straight.

"Oh, I—er—I didn't mean—er—anything against Harrison," answered Felix Merwell, hastily. "I think Endicott is deceiving him, that's all. But it is not his fault. I—er—suppose, though, I'll have to let the matter drop. Just the same, I think some of my cattle slipped into that drove." And there the matter rested. Mr. Merwell knew he was in the wrong, but he was too mean a man to acknowledge it. Truly, father and son were equally despicable.

"I wish he would sell out," said Belle, to the other girls. "But I am afraid he won't—he'll stay here just so he and Link can worry us."

"Maybe he wants you to sell out," said Jessie.

"Well, we'll not do it," answered Belle, with spirit.

On the following day the boys and girls went out on a picnic, taking a generous lunch with them. They persuaded Mr. and Mrs. Endicott to go along with them, and after they returned home the ranch owner and his wife said they felt ten years younger. They had joined in all the games played, helped to build a campfire and make coffee, and "cut up" just as if they were young themselves.

"Oh, if only papa and mamma were here!" sighed Jessie. "I must write them a long letter, telling them all about it!" And the letter was penned the next morning. On that day came a letter from Dunston Porter, stating he would stop at Star Ranch for them ten days from date.

"Only ten days more!" cried Dave. "My, how the time flies!"

There was also a letter from Nat Poole, in which Nat stated

that he had been looking for the fellow who called himself Tom Shocker and had at last located the rascal in a town not far from Buffalo. He had accused the man of the robbery at the hotel, and caused the fellow to give up the stickpin and also a pawn-ticket for the watch. The timepiece had been recovered, and both articles were now at the Wadsworth home, waiting for Dave.

"Well, I am glad Nat got the things back," said Dave.

"Maybe that will be a lesson to him, not to trust strangers in the future," was Phil's comment. "But how about the money?"

"Nat says Shocker spent that."

"Then Nat will have to make it good," said Roger.

"Yes, he says he will," answered Dave.

"What about that grand hunt we were to have?" questioned Roger. "Only ten days more, remember."

"I'll see Todd about it at once," was Dave's answer.

The matter was talked over, not only with the cowboy, but with the others, and it was finally decided that the boys and Todd should leave the ranch home two days later, for a hunt that was to last three and possibly four days. They were to go on horseback, and carry with them a small tent and a fair supply of provisions, as well as two rifles and their shotguns, and the cowboy's pistol.

"We'll strike out straight for the mountains," said Todd. "To be sure, we may find some game in the hills close by, but in the mountains we'll be certain to run down something worth while."

"Well, you look out that something doesn't run you down—a bear, for instance," said Laura.

"Boys that can kill a bobcat can kill a bear, if they try," answered Sid Todd.

The boys were in great delight, and spent every minute of their time in getting ready for the trip. Guns were cleaned and oiled, and they sorted and packed their ammunition with care. Mr. Endicott had a compact camping outfit, consisting of dishes and cooking utensils, and the little tent, and these were made into convenient packs for the horses, and the provisions were likewise strapped up properly. Todd aided in all, and the lads had to admire how deftly he put things together so that they might be carried with comparative ease.

"He has been there before, that is plain to see," said the senator's son.

"A fine man," declared Dave, heartily. "I shall feel perfectly safe with him along."

The girls were sorry to see the boys go, yet every one of them wished the lads the best of luck.

"Please don't run into any danger!" pleaded Jessie.

"Don't shoot at a bear unless you know you can get away from him if you miss him," cautioned Laura.

"And, above all, don't get lost in the mountains," was Belle's advice.

It had looked like rain the night before, and the boys were worried, not wishing to depart in the wet. But the sun came out full in the morning, and their spirits at once arose. Roger could not contain himself and whistled merrily, while Phil did a double shuffle while waiting for breakfast. Dave was also happy, although sorry that the girls, and especially Jessie, would not be along.

"All ready!" cried Todd, half an hour later, when the horses had been brought around to the piazza.

"I am!" cried Dave.

"So am I," came from Phil and Roger.

"Then good-by, everybody!" shouted the cowboy, swinging his sombrero, and off he galloped. The boys said farewell, the girls waved their handkerchiefs, one of the hands fired off his pistol, and away the lads went after Todd; and the grand hunt was begun.

It was still early and delightfully cool, with a faint breeze blowing from the distant mountains, for which they were headed. Todd had already told them that they were to keep on steadily until exactly noon, crossing the river, and following a brook that came from the upper hills.

"I know a fine spot to stop for dinner," he said. "And we can make it if you'll keep up with me." He always took his dinner at noon, having no use for "lunch" at any time.

On and on over the smooth plains the party galloped, and by the middle of the forenoon reached the river.

"No use in stopping for a mess of fish, I suppose," said the senator's son, wistfully.

"You can catch 'em up in the hills just as well," answered the cowboy. "Sweeter, too, maybe," he added. Many fishermen think that the higher up a stream you go for fish, the sweeter they are to the taste.

The cowboy had certainly set a smart pace, but none of the boys grumbled, for they were as anxious as he to reach the mountains and look for game.

"Of course you can keep your eyes open around here," he said, as they galloped along. "But you won't see much, I'm afraid."

"I see some grouse!" cried the shipowner's son, a few minutes later. "We might bring some of those down and cook them for supper. We won't want to wait to do it for dinner."

He pointed to some grouse far away, and all agreed that the fowls would make good eating. They rode behind some bushes, tied their horses, and went forward with caution. All fired together, and when the smoke cleared away they saw that four of the game had been laid low. The rest had flown away, and to follow them would have been useless.

"Well, four are all right!" cried Roger, and was about to rush forward to pick up the grouse when of a sudden Dave yelled to him to stop.

"What's the matter?" asked the senator's son.

"A snake!" screamed Phil. And as he spoke all in the party saw what Dave had first discovered. A rattlesnake had appeared from a hole in a tree, close to where the dead grouse lay!

CHAPTER XXVI

AFTER DEER

"A rattlesnake!"

"Take care that he doesn't bite you!"

"My, what a big fellow!"

"He is heading this way!"

Such were some of the cries uttered by the young hunters and Sid Todd as all beheld a large-sized snake crawling from a hole under the tree. That it was a rattler there was no doubt.

All leaped back, for the sight momentarily stunned them. But then Dave recovered his presence of mind and blazed away with his shotgun, hitting the reptile in the middle, and inflicting several ugly but not mortal wounds. The rattlesnake gave a hiss, glided under some leafy bushes, and there commenced to sound his rattles.

"He's going to strike!" cried Phil, and as he spoke the shotgun in Sid Todd's hands was discharged. He fired among the leaves, and whether or not he hit the snake, nobody could tell.

"Don't go near him," called out Roger. He hated snakes about as much as he hated anything.

All waited, and while doing so, Dave and Todd took the opportunity to reload. They were just finishing when Phil, chancing to look behind them, uttered a yell that would have done credit to an Apache Indian.

"Look out! One of 'em is behind us!"

The others all took his word for it, and leaped to one side. True enough, a second rattlesnake had appeared, and now a third was coming to light, from under a rock near by.

"It's a den of rattlers!" screamed Sid Todd. "Run for it, boys! No use of trying to kill 'em off! They are too many for us!"

The boys were already running at top speed, and the cowboy joined them. In order to gain the horses, they had to move in a semicircle. When they reached the animals, they found the steeds exceedingly nervous and inclined to bolt.

"Reckon they smell the snakes," was Todd's comment. "A hoss ain't got no use for rattlers—and I ain't nuther," he added, and rode away, with the boys beside him.

"What about the grouse?" asked Phil, mournfully.

"Do you want to go back after them?" questioned Dave, with a grim smile.

"Not for a thousand dollars!"

"Then I guess we'll have to let the snakes have them," went on Dave. "Let us be thankful that we weren't bitten."

"Rattlesnakes is the one drawback to this country," said the cowboy, when they were a safe distance from the reptiles. "I don't mind wild beasts, but I do draw the line on snakes. But there ain't near so many as there used to be, an' some day there won't be any at all."

"After this I am going to beware of holes that look snaky," was Roger's comment. "I think if a rattlesnake got close to me I'd be paralyzed with fright."

As they went on, they kept their eyes open for more game, and just before resting for dinner Dave saw some grouse high up in a tree in a hollow. With caution they advanced, this time on horseback, and all fired together as before. Out of the tree fluttered seven grouse, for they had been close together and the shot had created great havoc. All but one were dead and the seventh was quickly dispatched by Todd.

"We'll have some good eating to-night, after all," said Roger, with a grin. He liked fowl of all kinds.

The stop for dinner was made beside a mountain spring, where the water was icy cold and as clear as crystal. They took their time eating, thus allowing the horses a chance to rest and to crop the nearby grass.

"We have covered about twenty miles," said the cowboy, in reply to a question from Phil.

"Then, if we do as well this afternoon, we'll be forty miles from the ranch by the time we camp to-night."

"We'll not make over ten or twelve miles this afternoon, lad," was the answer. "It will be hard climbing up the hills."

"But harder climbing to-morrow," put in Dave.

"Yes, to-morrow will test the horses, and test you, too," said Todd.

It was very pleasant to rest in the shade after such a long ride in the sun, but the cowboy was anxious to reach a certain camping spot for the night, and so he allowed only three-quarters of an hour for the midday halt.

As soon as they left the spring, the youths realized what was before them. The trail now led constantly upward, and was in parts stony and uncertain. In several places they had to leap brooks of fair size.

"This isn't so nice," remarked Phil, as they came to a halt, to allow the horses to rest after a particularly difficult hill had been climbed.

"Oh, this is nothing to the traveling we'll do to-morrow," answered Sid Todd. "We are only in the foothills now—to-morrow we'll be right in the mountains."

About four o'clock they gained the top of another hill. As they came out in a cleared spot all gazed around with interest.

"Look!" cried Dave, pointing with his hand. "Am I mistaken, or are those deer?"

He was pointing to the top of another hill about half a mile distant. There, outlined against the sky, could be seen a number of animals grazing.

"Deer, my boy!" cried Sid Todd. "A fine lot of 'em, too, or I'm mistaken!"

"Oh, let us go after them!" exclaimed Roger, impulsively.

"I'm willing," answered the cowboy. "But I don't know if you can get any of 'em to-night. It will be a hard climb to where they are. I don't know as we can go all the way on hosses."

"Then we'll go on foot," cried Dave. He was as anxious as his chums to get a shot at the big game.

The cowboy studied the situation for several minutes, meanwhile withdrawing himself and the others to a spot where the distant deer might not see them. Then he led the party down the hill and in the direction of the game.

If traveling had been hard before, it was doubly so now, and the chums realized that to get to where the deer were grazing would be no easy matter. They had to slip and slide over the rocks, and once or twice they reached places where further progress seemed impossible.

"If we get any of those deer, we'll earn them!" panted Phil, as he half climbed, half slid, over some rocks. "If my horse goes down, I don't know what will happen to me!" he added.

"We'll not go much further on hossback, I'm thinking," answered Todd. "We can't afford to injure our animals."

Between the hills was a small valley and here the cowboy said they had better tether their steeds and leave them.

"Even if we don't get back, they'll likely be safe till morning," he added.

"If we have to remain away all night, we had better take some eating with us," said Phil.

"We sure will," answered Todd, and he gave each of the party something to carry on his back and in his gamebag.

"Now for a climb that is a climb!" cried Dave. "Roger, this puts me in mind of some climbing I did in Norway."

"Were you in Norway?" questioned Sid Todd, curiously.

"Oh, yes, I once went there to find my father," answered Dave.

Before them was a steep incline, covered with stones and a stunted growth of cedars. Up this they went with care, for some of the stones were loose and afforded only an uncertain footing. Once Phil slipped and commenced to roll. He bumped against Dave, and both went flat.

"Grab a tree!" sang out Roger. But there was no need to offer this advance, for Dave had already done so. He saved himself and Phil from rolling further. But a frying-pan the shipowner's son carried broke loose from the pack on his back and went clattering down the rocks to the very foot of the hill.

"For the love of flapjacks, stop that noise!" cried Sid Todd, in a low voice. "Time you get to the top of the hill them deer will be ten miles away!"

"I—I couldn't help it," answered Phil, as he arose and gazed sorrowfully after the frying-pan. "Shall I go back after it?" he asked.

"Where is it?"

"I see it—sticking in the fork of a cedar tree," answered Roger, and pointed out the pan.

"Let it alone—we can get it when we come back," said the cowboy. "Now don't make any more noise, or you won't get no chanct at them deer, mark my words!"

All of the boys understood the importance of keeping quiet, and as they neared the top of the hill where the deer had been discovered, they moved with great caution and spoke only in whispers.

"The wind is blowing toward us, and that's in our favor," said Sid Todd.

"I know it," answered Dave. "Deer can scent a fellow a long way off if the wind is towards them."

The cowboy now took the lead and told the lads not to make a sound that was unnecessary. Thus they covered another hundred yards. Here was a ridge of rocks and beyond the top of the hill.

"They are gone!" murmured Roger, as his eyes discovered that the top of the hill was abandoned.

"I'll crawl forward and take a look," said Todd. "Keep quiet now, or we won't git nuthin'."

The cowboy disappeared over the top of the hill, crawling forward on his hands and knees. He was gone fully ten minutes—a time that to the boys, just then, seemed like an age. They looked to their weapons, to see that the firearms were ready for use.

Presently Dave, who was on the watch, saw Todd arise in a clump of bushes on the other side of the hilltop. He was beckoning for the boys to advance. One hand he held over his mouth, to enjoin silence.

With their hearts beating more rapidly than usual, the three young hunters wormed their way over the top of the hill and joined the cowboy. In silence Todd pointed to a distance below them. There, on a sort of cliff on the hillside, were the deer, ten in number, grazing peacefully.

"Oh, what a shot!" whispered Dave, and his eyes brightened as he swung his gun into position.

"Wait!" said Todd, in a whisper. "I'll take the one on the right. You take the one on the left."

"I'll take the one close to the tree," whispered the senator's son.

"And I'll take the one by the big rock," added Phil.

"All right," agreed the cowboy. "Now, remember, if some are only wounded, shoot at 'em again, any one of you. And be quick, for they'll streak it like greased lightning as soon as the guns go off."

All took aim with care, resting their gun-barrels on the bushes before them. Then the cowboy gave the order to fire.

As if by instinct the deer looked up just as the order to fire was given. They were fairly close to hand and afforded good targets for the hunters. The firearms rang out almost simultaneously, and two of the deer leaped into the air, to fall back dead. The others started to run, some jumping from the top of the cliff to the rocks far below. Again the weapons were discharged, and this time a third deer fell. The fourth was badly wounded and toppled down in a split of the cliff.

"Hurrah! we've got 'em! We've got 'em!" cried Phil, and commenced to leap about in pure joy.

"We've got 'em—to get!" answered Sid Todd. "But you did well—all of you!" he added, admiringly.

"How are we to get down to the cliff?" questioned Roger, anxiously.

"The deer got down—we had better follow their trail," answered Dave.

They made an examination, and presently found a run leading to one end of the cliff. The walking was dangerous and they had to be careful, for fear of going further than intended. But inside of a quarter of an hour all were standing where the deer had stood. They found three of the game dead and quickly put the fourth out of its misery.

"This is worth coming for," declared Dave, with pride.

"It is indeed—even if we don't get anything else," added Phil.

"But we are going to get more," cried Roger, the fever of the hunter taking possession of him. "Just wait till we strike an elk, or a bear!"

"No more hunting this day," sang out Todd. "Time we take care of these animals and make a camp it will be dark."

Edward Stratemeyer

CHAPTER XXVII

THE MOUNTAIN LION

"What are we to do with so much venison?" questioned the senator's son. "We can't eat it, and it seems a shame to allow it to go to waste."

"I wish we could send some to the ranch," said Dave. "I'd like the girls to know how lucky we have been the first day out."

"If you wanted to stay here and camp for a day, I could take some of the game to the ranch," said Sid Todd.

"But it is such a ride," argued Phil. "We don't want to impose on good nature."

"I won't mind the ride. But can you boys take care of yourselves while I am gone?"

"To be sure we can," answered Dave.

"Then I'll take three of the deer with me and come back as soon as I can. One deer will be all you will need," answered Sid Todd.

To get the deer from the cliff they had to use a long lariat the cowboy had brought with him. By this means the game was hoisted to the hilltop. Then they "toted" their loads down to where they had left their horses.

"I'll take two of the hosses, if you don't mind," said the cowboy, and it was agreed that he should take Dave's animal along with his own. He decided to start for the ranch that night, stating he would camp at the spot where they had had dinner.

The boys found a locality that pleased them, and there erected the tent and started a campfire. The frying-pan had been recovered from where it had landed and restored to the outfit. Before leaving them, Todd showed the boys how to skin the deer and cut up the meat.

For a little while after they were left alone the chums felt somewhat lonely. They piled the wood on the fire, thereby creating a lively blaze, and fixed themselves a substantial meal of venison steak, flapjacks and coffee, and took their time over the repast. By the time they had finished, night had fallen over the hills and mountains, and one by one the stars showed themselves in the heavens.

"This certainly is Lonesomehurst!" was the comment of the shipowner's son, as he gazed around the camp. "When you really get to think of it, it gives one the shivers!"

"Then don't think about it," answered Dave. "Let us be cheerful and tell ghost stories. I know a dandy story—about four travelers who were murdered in some lonely mountains by brigands, and—"

"You shut up!" cried Roger. "Don't you want a fellow to sleep to-night?"

"But I thought you wanted me to tell a story," went on Dave, innocently.

"I don't want to listen to such a story as that!"

"Nor do I!" added Phil. "Let's talk about schooldays, and the last game of football, or baseball, or something like that."

"If only the other fellows were here," murmured Dave. "Shadow Hamilton, and Buster Beggs, and Polly Vane, and Luke Watson, and—"

"Luke could give us a tune on his banjo," put in the senator's son.

"Yes, and Shadow would tell funny stories, not ghost stories," added Phil.

"We'll have a story or two to tell, when we get back to Oak Hall," continued Dave. "I wish we could have had one of the deer stuffed for the museum."

"Too late now. But maybe we'll get another," answered Phil.

All of the boys were tired, yet it was nearly ten o'clock before any of them felt like turning in. As the night wore on the place seemed to become more lonely.

"Might as well go to bed," said Dave, at last. "We need a good rest."

"Anybody going to stay on guard?" asked the senator's son.

"Do you think it necessary, Roger?"

"I don't know."

"What do you say, Phil?"

"I am too sleepy now to remain on guard," answered Phil. "You can do so if you wish."

"Oh, what cheek!" murmured Roger. "All right, we'll all turn in and chance it."

"Let's fix the fire first," said Dave. "A blaze usually helps to keep away wild beasts."

"Oh, if any come, I reckon the horses will give us warning," said Phil. "We can tie them close by." And this plan was carried out.

Some cedar boughs had been strewn on the floor of the tent, and on these the chums laid down, and did their best to go to sleep. Dave dropped off first, and was presently followed by Roger. But Phil was restless and turned from one side to the other.

"Oh, pshaw! why can't I sleep?" murmured the shipowner's son to himself in disgust, and then out of curiosity he looked at his watch. By the glare from the campfire he saw that it was nearly one o'clock.

He was just straightening out again when a peculiar rustling among the horses caught his ears. He listened for a moment, then sat up straight.

"Something doesn't suit them," he reasoned. "Wonder what it can be?"

He hesitated, then turned over on his hands and knees and crawled to the opening of the tent and peered around outside. The campfire had burned rather low, so that objects a short distance away were indistinct. He saw that the horses were huddled together and had their heads turned toward a clump of bushes at one side of the shelter.

"Something must be over yonder," reasoned the youth. "Wonder if I had better arouse the others?"

He looked at Dave and Roger. Both were sleeping so peacefully Phil hated to disturb them. He reached for his gun and looked out again.

There was a brushing aside of the clump of bushes and a pair of eyes glared forth, glistening brightly in the firelight. The eyes were those of some wild beast, but what, Phil could not tell.

The animal was not looking at Phil, but at the carcass of the deer, which had been hung up in a low tree not far from the clump of bushes. Stealthily the animal came into the opening, and with the ease of a cat, leaped into the tree.

"It's a wildcat—or something like it," thought Phil, and raised his gun to fire. Then of a sudden he commenced to shake from head to foot, so that to aim was entirely out of the question. He had what is commonly called among hunters "buck fever," a sudden fear that often overtakes amateur hunters when trying to shoot at big game.

"Oh, what a fool I am!" the boy told himself, and tried vainly to steady his nerves. He hit the front tent pole with his foot, making considerable noise.

"What's the matter?" cried Dave, waking and leaping to his feet. "What are you doing, Phil?"

"Noth—nothing," stammered the shipowner's son. "I—I—there is something in the tree!" And then, raising his gun, Phil banged away blindly.

The echo of the shot was followed by an unearthly scream from the tree, and Phil and Dave saw the wild animal slip down from a branch and then try to regain its footing. Then Dave caught up one of the rifles and blazed away, and the beast dropped to the ground, where it twisted and snarled and yelped in a fashion that served to drive the horses frantic.

"What's going on?" cried Roger, sitting up and rubbing his eyes. "Who is shooting?" And he got up and felt around in a haphazard manner for a gun.

"Wild animal outside—I don't know what it is," answered Dave.

Roger joined the others, and blazed away at the beast, and more snapping and snarling followed. The animal rolled clear over the fire, scattering the burning brands in all directions. Then it rolled among the horses. One steed after another kicked at it, and a flying hoof sent it against the tree with a thud. Then it lay quiet.

"Must be dead," said Dave, after a pause.

"Don't go near it!" screamed Phil.

"I won't—not yet," answered Dave. "We'll fix up the fire first." And he kicked the dying embers together and put more wood on the blaze. While he did this, Phil and Roger watched the huddled-up form at the foot of the tree. The horses still snorted and did their best to get away.

"I guess it is dead after all," said Phil, after he had poked the beast with a stick. "Wonder what it can be?"

"Looks a little like a big wildcat," said Roger.

"I know what it is," answered Dave, after all were certain the beast was dead and they had dragged it over to the fire. "It's a cougar, or mountain lion,—one of the worst wild beasts to be found in the West."

"Then it's no wonder I got scared when first I saw it," said Phil. "My, what a powerful animal! And it must weigh fifty or sixty pounds."

"All of that, Phil."

"Is this the beast some call a panther or painter?" asked Roger.

"Yes, Roger. I was reading about them in a natural history, and the cougar, mountain lion, puma, panther, and painter are all the same beast. Years ago they were common all over the United States, but now they are to be found only in the Far

West and in the South. I think we can count it a big feather in our cap that we killed a cougar."

"Do you think he was going to attack us?" asked the senator's son, with a shiver.

"He was after the deer. But there is no telling what he might have done. I am glad he is dead. Phil, it was lucky you heard the beast."

"Talk about excitement!" cried the shipowner's son. "I rather think we are getting it! Rattlesnakes, deer, and a panther, all in one day and night!"

"That is certainly piling it on some," admitted Dave. "But to-morrow may pass without a thing doing."

"More than likely," returned Roger. "Things always happen in bunches, you know."

The boys examined the cougar with interest. It was about four and a half feet in length and not unlike a young lion in appearance. It had been hit in the face and in the forelegs, and had died hard. Evidently it had hoped to carry off the slain deer while the young hunters slept.

"A cougar has been known to carry off a little child," said Dave. "They are very crafty as well as brave, and will attack both a horse and a man. I think we can count ourselves lucky to come out of this fight without a scratch."

"No more sleeping for me without a guard," said Roger. "Let us take turns at staying up and looking after the fire and the horses." And to this the others readily agreed.

Morning found them still tired out and willing enough to rest. They got a late breakfast and tethered the horses in a new spot, and cut sufficient firewood to last for twenty-four hours. Nobody thought of doing anything until after lunch, and then

Roger suggested they try their hand at fishing in a mountain brook which ran down between the two hills.

"All right," answered Dave. "But do you think we ought to leave the camp all alone?"

"Oh, I don't think anybody will hurt it in the daylight," answered the senator's son.

They had to tramp about a quarter of a mile to reach the stream and then an equal distance to gain a spot that looked suited to their purpose. Phil was the first to throw in, and was rewarded almost immediately by a bite.

"This looks as if it was worth while," said Dave, and baited up. Fish were there in plenty, and for an hour the boys amused themselves to their hearts' content. By that time each had a string of fifteen to twenty mountain brook trout of fair size.

"We'll have a dandy fish supper!" cried Roger, smacking his lips.

"It will be a change from the venison, and I'll be glad of it," returned Dave.

"I am going to try my luck for a short while up the stream," called out Phil, who was some distance away from the others.

"Don't go too far," said Dave. "I am going to rest here," and he threw himself on the grass, and Roger followed his example.

The two boys left behind rested for the best part of half an hour. Then, thinking it was time for Phil to rejoin them, they called their chum's name.

No answer came back, and, walking up the stream a short distance, Dave repeated the call. Still there was no reply.

"That's queer," he told Roger. "I wonder why he doesn't reply?"

"I am sure I don't know," said the senator's son. "Let us look for him." And both started after Phil, wondering what could be wrong.

CHAPTER XXVIII

UP TO THE MOUNTAIN TOP

Dave and Roger walked up the stream a distance of several hundred yards. They continued to call Phil's name, but as before, no answer came back.

"I must confess, Roger, I don't like the looks of things," said Dave, gravely. "If Phil was all right, he'd surely answer us."

"I think so myself, Dave—unless he was only fooling us."

"I don't think he'd do that, under the circumstances. He'd know we would be greatly worried."

On walked the two chums, until they reached a point where the mountain stream came tumbling over some great rocks. Here they found Phil's fishing rod and also the string of fish he had caught.

"Gracious, Dave! Supposing some wild animal has carried him off!" ejaculated the senator's son.

Dave did not reply, for he knew not what to say. He advanced to the top of the rocks and peered over on the other side.

"There he is!" he shouted. "Phil! Phil! Are you hurt?" he called.

Only a faint moan came back, and scrambling up the rocks

Edward Stratemeyer

beside Dave, Roger saw the trouble. Phil had slipped from the rocks into the mountain torrent. In going down his legs had caught in an opening below, and there he was held, in water up to his knees, while the water from some rocks above was pouring in a steady stream over his left shoulder.

"Can't you get up, Phil?" asked Dave.

"Hel—help!" was the only answer, delivered in such a low tone that the boys on the rocks could scarcely hear it.

"He can't aid himself, that is sure," murmured Dave. "Roger, we have got to get him out of that—before that water pouring over his shoulder carries him down!"

Both boys looked around anxiously. Phil was all of fifteen feet below them and there seemed to be no way of reaching the locality short of jumping, and neither wanted to risk doing that.

"If we only had a rope," said Roger.

"We might double up a fishing line," mused Dave. Then his face brightened. "I have it—the pole!"

He ran back and speedily brought up Phil's pole, and around it he wound the line, to strengthen it and hold the joints together. Then he leaned down.

"Phil, can you take hold?" he questioned.

The youth below raised his hands feebly. But his strength was apparently gone, and he could do little to save himself.

"Hold the pole, Dave, I'll go down!" cried Roger. "But don't let me slip!"

While Dave braced himself on the rocks as best he could and gripped the pole and line, the senator's son went over the rocks and down, hand over hand. This was easy, and in a minute he stood beside Phil in the water. The torrent from above poured over his back, but to this he paid no attention. He saw that Phil was on the point of fainting, and if he sank down he would surely be drowned.

Letting go his hold on the fishing pole, Roger felt down in the water, and then discovered that Phil's feet were crossed and held by a rock that was balanced on another rock. In coming down, Phil's weight had caused the space between the two rocks to widen, then the opening had partly closed, holding the feet as if in the jaws of some big animal.

It was no easy matter for Roger to shift the upper rock, and once he slipped and went flat on his back in the water with a loud splash.

"Be careful!" warned Dave from above. "Maybe I had better come down and help you," he added.

"No, I—I'm all ri—right!" spluttered the senator's son, freeing his mouth of water.

At last one of the rocks was moved and Phil staggered forward in the water. But he was too weak to help himself and had to lean on Roger.

"You can't pull us up!" shouted the senator's son. "We'll wade down the stream a bit."

Supporting the shipowner's son, Roger commenced to move down the mountain torrent. He had to pick his way with care, for the bottom was rocky and treacherous. Dave followed along the rocks above, until a spot was gained where he could leap down. Then he and the senator's son picked up Phil between them and carried him out, and up to a patch of grass, where they set the sufferer down in the sunlight.

"We'll take off his shoes and see how his feet and ankles look," said Dave, and this was done. They found the feet and ankles slightly swollen and discolored, but not seriously injured.

"Phil, supposing Roger and I carry you back to camp?" suggested Dave. "We can make an armchair and do it easily enough."

"If it isn't too much trouble I'd be glad to have you do it," answered the boy who had slipped over the rocks. "I can't walk yet."

The chums had often carried each other "armchair fashion" while at school, and soon Dave and Roger started off with Phil between them, and carrying the fishing pole and fish. On the way they rested several times and also gathered up their own outfits and catches.

Arriving at the camp, the fire was stirred up, and the lads hung up the most of their clothing to dry, while they took a good rubbing-down. Phil's feet and ankles were bathed in hot water and then soaked in some liniment Mrs. Endicott had made them bring along in case of accident. The injured lad was content to rest on a bed of cedar boughs, but declared that he would be as well as ever in the morning.

"But I am mighty glad you came when you did," he said, with deep feeling. "I could not have held up much longer—with that stream of water rushing down over my shoulder. I yelled and yelled, until I couldn't yell any longer."

"That must have been before we started to look for you," returned Dave. "After this you want to be careful how you climb around. Some of the rocks are loose and very treacherous."

Dave and Roger prepared a fine supper of broiled fish, and to this meal even Phil did full justice. As there was nothing else to do, the boys took their time eating. They had almost finished when they heard a shout from a distance.

"What's that?" cried Roger, and instinctively he leaped up and moved for his gun.

"It's Todd!" answered Dave. "Hello, Todd!" he yelled. "This way!"

The others joined in the cry, which was answered from a distance, and presently the cowboy appeared on his horse and leading Dave's animal.

"I reckon I'm just in time for a fish supper!" he cried, with a broad smile on his face. "Well, I'm hungry enough, with such a stiff ride. What's the matter with your feet?" he questioned, gazing at Phil's bandages.

The boys told the story of the trouble up the stream, and then related how they had shot the cougar, and exhibited the body of the slain beast. In the meantime they broiled some more fish, and made an extra pot of coffee and some flapjacks for the newcomer.

"Well! well! well!" cried Sid Todd, after a look at the dead cougar. "I reckon you youngsters know how to take care of yourselves. A mountain lion! Why, don't you know, most o' the cowboys would run a mile if they see that beast a-lookin' at' em? Such shootin' is great!"

"Well, we don't want to meet any more of them," answered Dave.

"No, the rest of them can keep their distance," added Phil.

"Did you get the deer home all right?" questioned Roger.

"Oh, yes, and the folks were a good deal surprised and pleased. The girls are going to have one of the deer stuffed and mounted, for the Wadsworth home. They said it would please Mr. Wadsworth and Professor—let me see—I reckon it's Professor Pans."

"No, Professor Potts," said Dave.

"Well, I knew it had something to do with cookin'-things," answered the cowboy. "Mr. Endicott told me to be careful and tell you not to shoot everything there was in the mountains, as he wanted to come out later for a shot or two."

"I guess there will be enough left after we get through," said Dave, with a smile.

The cowboy had had a hard ride and he was willing enough to eat his supper in peace. Then he smoked a pipe of tobacco and turned in. He said the boys could keep a guard if they wished, but he scarcely deemed it necessary.

"Won't another mountain lion, or anything else, come around in a year," said he. "That jest happened that way, that's all." And after some talk among themselves the chums concluded to turn in, all hands, and let the camp and the horses take care of themselves.

The night passed quietly and all slept until the sun was well up in the heavens. Then, while the boys prepared breakfast and Phil attended to his bruised feet—which felt much better—Sid Todd told of some happenings at the ranch.

"The girls went out for a horseback ride, along with Mrs. Endicott," said he, "and, coming back, they met Link Merwell. They said he acted so disagreeable that they were afraid of him. Mrs. Endicott was very angry, and I think the boss will speak to Mr. Merwell about it."

"Link ought to be hammered good and hard!" cried Roger.

"The boss wishes the Merwells would sell out. But Mr. Merwell doesn't seem to want to budge. The girls were so afraid of Link they said they wouldn't go out again unless Mr. Endicott was along," continued the cowboy.

"If he molests the girls, he'll have another account to settle with me!" cried Dave.

"And me!" came promptly from his chums.

"He wanted to know where you fellows were, and said he was going out hunting himself."

"He needn't come near us," cried the senator's son. "We don't want him."

"Oh, he won't come near us—unless to make trouble, you may be sure of that," answered Dave.

The cowboy had left word at Star Ranch that the young hunters might remain out longer than originally intended, so the chums did not worry about getting back. All rested during the morning, and after dinner started on the trail up into the mountains.

"How is it, Phil?" asked Dave, on the way.

"Oh, I can ride very well," was the reply. "But I am rather glad I haven't much walking to do. But I think I'll be O.K. by to-morrow."

Sid Todd had been right about the climbing to be done during the last stage of the journey, and often the boys, as they looked ahead at the rocks before them, wondered how they were going to make progress. But the cowboy knew the trail, and up they went, the scenery every moment growing wilder and more impressive.

"This is an ideal spot for wild animals," said Dave. "I should think hunting would be very good."

Once they stopped to let the horses rest. They were out on a cliff and at a distance Sid Todd pointed out two nests perched up on the top of rocky crags. The nests were several feet in diameter.

"What are they?" questioned Dave.

"Eagles' nests," was the answer. "There are two of the eagles now," and the cowboy pointed out the big birds, floating lazily around between two distant mountain tops.

"A fellow would have difficulty in getting to those nests," was Phil's comment.

"Eagles usually build where nobody can git at 'em," returned Todd.

"I shouldn't care to shoot an eagle," said Dave. "Somehow, I'd feel a good deal as if I had shot at our flag."

"I think I'd feel that way, too," answered the senator's son.

"The eagle and Old Glory seem to be linked together," added Phil. "But I wouldn't mind catching a young eagle and taming him."

"You'd have your hands full doing it," said Sid Todd. "I know a cowboy who once caught an eagle, but the bird scratched him terribly and nearly took off one of his ears."

On they went again, until, an hour later, they gained the top of the mountain. Here they found a stiff breeze blowing, and it was much cooler than below.

"I see some game!" cried Dave, and pointed to a slope on the other side of the mountain. Two deer were in view.

Scarcely had Dave spoken when a shot rang out and one of the deer jumped as if hit. The other ran off and disappeared in the bushes. Then, slowly and painfully, the second deer limped away. A second shot rent the air, but the wounded animal was not touched, and a second later it followed its mate to cover.

CHAPTER XXIX

TWO ELK AND A BEAR

"I guess that hunter, whoever he is, will lose that deer," was Dave's comment.

"He won't if he knows how to follow the game up," answered Sid Todd. "That deer was badly wounded, and game can't run far over these rough rocks."

"Wonder who it was?" mused Phil.

"Can't tell that—so many folks come out here to hunt," answered the cowboy. "It might be some ranchman or cowboy, and it might be some city sportsman trying his luck."

"We may fall in with him later," said Dave. "If we do, I hope he proves a nice sort."

"Folks out here usually hunt on their own hook," said Todd.

The cowboy had in mind to pass to the north of the mountain top, and this they did, soon leaving behind the locality where the two deer had been seen. They saw nothing of the party who had fired the two shots.

"I hope he doesn't take us for game and shoot this way," said Roger, who had heard of just such accidents more than once.

238   Edward Stratemeyer

"Well, we don't want to mistake him for game either," said Dave. "Whenever you shoot, be sure of what you are shooting at."

"Right you are," cried Sid Todd. "If hunters weren't too hasty there wouldn't be any accidents."

A little over half a mile was covered, and by that time the sun was sinking over the hills to the westward. A suitable spot was selected and the tent was pitched, and they prepared a supper of fish and venison, meat and crackers, washing it down with some chocolate that Roger made.

Early in the morning Sid Todd left the camp, to be gone the best part of two hours. He came back showing his excitement.

"A chance for elk, boys!" he cried. "But you must hurry and do a good bit of tramping."

"Can you walk, Phil?" asked Dave, anxiously.

"Just as well as ever," was the answer, and Phil took a turn around the camp to prove his words.

No time was lost in preparing for the hunt, and in less than ten minutes all were off, having tethered the horses in a spot they deemed safe. Their provisions they tied in skins and hung in the trees, so they might be safe from wild marauders.

It was a hard climb, over the rocks and among the bushes, and once the boys had to call a halt, to catch their breath. But Todd was afraid the elk would take themselves off, so he urged them on as much as possible.

"There were two elk, big fellows, too," he said. "If we don't bag at least one of 'em, we may not get another such chance all the time we are out here."

Presently they came to something of a hollow on the mountain side. Here was a fine spring of sparkling water, and all stopped long enough to get a refreshing drink. It was hot in the sun and all were beginning to perspire freely.

"If we get those elk we'll earn 'em," was Roger's comment.

"Right you are!" panted Phil.

"How much further have we to go?" questioned Dave.

"Not over a quarter of a mile," answered the cowboy. He was still in the lead and he had his eyes on the alert for the first glimpse at the big game.

The boys were pretty well winded when Sid Todd called a halt. They had reached a clump of cedar trees and beyond was an open spot among a number of loose rocks, with patches of rich mountain grass between.

"Gone!" said the cowboy, with a deep sigh.

"Gone!" echoed the three boys, in dismay.

"Yes, gone. They were right out yonder, grazing as peacefully as could be. Now I don't see 'em anywhere," continued the cowboy, mournfully.

"It's too bad!" murmured Dave. "Maybe you would have done better if you had fired on them."

"I wanted you lads to have a chance."

"Perhaps they are still in this vicinity," suggested Roger. "Let us take a look around."

The others were willing, and slowly and cautiously they made their way among the cedars and the big rocks, exposing themselves as little as possible, and speaking only in a whisper. They had the rifles and shotguns ready for action.

Edward Stratemeyer

Half an hour's search took them to another dent in the mountain side. Here the grass was extra thick and inviting and a spring of water flowed quietly over the rocks.

"That's an ideal spot for a camp," said Phil to Dave, as they halted to view the scene.

Dave did not answer, for he had seen something moving in the bushes close to the water. He pointed in silence, and all gazed in the direction. Slowly a magnificent pair of antlers arose behind the bushes.

"One of the elk!" whispered Sid Todd.

"And there is the other!" came from Roger, and pointed to a rock twenty yards beyond the bushes.

"Now, boys, be careful," directed the cowboy. "This is the chance of your lives. Divide up the game to suit yourselves. I won't shoot unless I see the elk getting away from you."

The chums consulted among themselves, and Roger and Phil decided to aim at the elk nearest to them.

"Then I'll aim at the elk near the rock," said Dave. "I think I've got the best rifle anyway," he added.

All crawled forward, followed by Todd, and thus covered half the distance toward the game. The nearest elk was now less than a hundred yards away.

"They see us!" cried Phil, and hastily raised his firearm, and the others did the same. Then, as the elk bounded away, all three of the young hunters fired.

Both the animals were hit, but neither mortally, and as soon as possible the boys fired a second time. The elk were now together, and a bullet and some shot meant for one hit the other. One of the animals staggered and fell, got up, and staggered again, coming down on the rocks with a loud thud.

"You've got this one!" cried Sid Todd, in triumph. "Go after the other!"

The boys were not loath to do this, and away they went pell-mell, over the grass and around the rocks and bushes. The second elk was limping along, occasionally holding his left hind leg in the air. He did not seem to be going fast, but he dodged in and out among the rocks so quickly that to get another shot at him seemed impossible.

"If we can only get him into the open we'll have him!" cried Dave.

The trail now led down the mountain side and then into a thicket of cedars. As they entered the thicket, Dave gave a yell.

"Look out!"

He leaped to one side and the other lads did the same. A second later the wounded elk rushed almost on them, his antlers lowered as if to crush all in his path. The boys fired as quickly as they could, and hit in the side, the animal swerved and dashed off at a right angle to the course he had been pursuing.

"Phew! but that was a narrow escape!" gasped Phil.

"It's different when the game hunts you, isn't it?" queried the senator's son.

"We must keep our eyes open, and our guns ready," said Dave. "Come ahead, that elk must be pretty hard hit by this time."

Again they went on. They could hear the big game crashing among the cedars. Evidently the elk was in such pain he did not know where to go.

"I see him!" cried Dave five minutes later, and pointed to a rocky elevation ahead. At the foot of the rocks stood the elk, glaring in rage at them. All of the young hunters elevated their firearms, and as they did this the big game charged them full tilt.

Crack! bang! crack! went the weapons, and the elk was halted in his course. He tried to come on, but in vain, and slowly swayed from side to side. Then he tried to retreat, but it was too late. With a snort he went over, kicking up big clods of grass as he did so. Then he gave a shiver and breathed his last.

"We've got him! We've got him!" cried Roger, exultantly, and began to caper about in his joy. "Just think of it, Dave, two elk! Isn't that something to be proud of?"

"I think so," answered Dave, his face beaming.

"I suppose the other elk is dead," said Phil. "But we'd better go back and make sure."

"We don't want to leave this here," said Roger, wistfully. "That other hunter might come along and claim him."

"I'll go back to where we left Todd, and you can watch this elk," said Dave. "I'll ask Todd what we had best do with both animals."

"Can you find the way?" questioned Phil.

"I think so."

Reloading his rifle, Dave set off for the spot where they had left the cowboy and the first elk. For a few minutes he followed the back trail with ease, then, almost before he was aware, he became mixed up and scarcely knew in what direction to turn.

"I suppose I might call out, or fire my rifle," he mused. "But if I do that the others may think I am in trouble."

Looking around carefully, Dave set off once more, and presently reached a spot that looked familiar. On the ground he could see footprints and these he commenced to follow. But in a few minutes he found himself in a thicket he was sure he had never seen before.

"I am mixed up, and no mistake," he murmured, his face falling. "I shouldn't have been so sure of myself at the start. It isn't so easy as one thinks to find a trail among these rocks and bushes. I guess I had better call to Todd, and to the others."

He set up a shout and waited for a reply. None came, and he shouted a second time. Then, from a distance, came a call.

"Well, I didn't think Todd was in that direction," he said to himself. "I am twisted and no mistake."

Again he started off, and this time found himself skirting a series of loose rocks of various sizes. He was going down hill and occasionally loosened a round stone with his foot and sent it crashing to a thicket of cedars below.

A hundred yards were covered when Dave heard the cry again. Now it was plainer, and it sounded a little like a call for help.

"Maybe Todd is in trouble," he mused. "Perhaps that elk got up and attacked him!" And with this thought in his mind he set off on a dog-trot in the direction of the voice he had heard.

It was dangerous among the loose stones, and once Dave went down and rolled over and over, coming pretty close to hitting his face and shooting off his rifle. As he picked himself up he heard a call quite plainly.

"Help! help! Somebody help me!"

"It must be Todd!" burst from the youth's lips, and now, in spite of the danger, he bounded from rock to rock down the slope. The call came from the left, and thither he made his way, halting in dismay as he came out on a little cliff.

At the foot of the cliff he saw the man who had uttered the call for aid. It was Hank Snogger. He was having a fierce face-to-face tussle with a big bear. His gun was on the ground and so was his sombrero, and in his hand he held his hunting knife. As Dave viewed the scene in horror, the bear made a pass with one forepaw and sent the hunting knife whirling from the cowboy's grasp. Then the bear closed in, as if to hug Snogger to death!

CHAPTER XXX

TO THE RESCUE—CONCLUSION

It was a time for quick action and nobody realized this more than did Dave, as he saw the shaggy brute close in on the cowboy. One squeeze of those powerful forepaws and Hank Snogger's ribs would be crushed in and he would be killed.

With hardly a second thought concerning what he was doing, Dave raised his rifle, took quick aim and fired at the bear. Then he fired a second shot, and followed this up with a third.

At the first shot the bear dropped his hold and swung around, uttering a loud snort of pain as he did so. He had been struck in the back, for the youth had not dared to aim too close to Snogger. Then, thinking that he had been hurt by the man before him, the animal made a leap and sent the cowboy sprawling. As he stood over his victim the second shot hit him in the hind quarters, causing him to whirl around. Then the third shot landed in his side, and made him double up like a ball and roll over and over.

"Kill him! Kill him!" came faintly from Hank Snogger. "Don't let him git at me ag'in!"

Dave tried to fire another shot, but for some reason then unknown the rifle refused to work. The bear was rolling over and over and threatened each instant to roll on the cowboy and crush him. Snogger was so weak he was unable to save

Edward Stratemeyer

himself or do anything in his own defense.

Dave glanced around and his eye fell on the loose stones, some of which had caused him a fall. He dropped his rifle, seized a fair-sized stone and hurled it at the bear. The youth's aim was good, and the missile landed on bruin's head, all but stunning him.

"That's it! Gi—give him ano—another!" gasped Hank Snogger. He had raised himself up on one elbow and was looking at Dave pleadingly. He was too weak to get to his feet, for his fight with the bear had lasted for some time before Dave had put in an appearance.

The boy from Crumville was not slow to pick up and throw another stone, and this took the bear in the side, causing him to grunt and snort in pain and rage. Then Dave got a stone of extra size and aimed again for the animal's head. The missile went true, and with his skull crushed, bruin stretched out and lay still.

"Is he—is he dead?" gasped Hank Snogger, hoarsely.

"I think so," answered Dave. He was trembling from the excitement and his breath came thick and fast.

"I—I thought I—I was done for!" added the cowboy, and sank flat on his back and closed his eyes.

Not without difficulty Dave got down to where the man lay. He found the bear stone dead and that the cowboy had fainted. He procured some water from a nearby brook and washed Snogger's face and soon revived the man. Then came a shout from a distance and Sid Todd showed himself, having been attracted to the spot by the rifle shots.

The situation was explained, and Dave came in for a good deal of praise over the killing of the bear.

"You saved my life!" said Hank Snogger. "I shan't forget it, never!" and he gave the youth a grateful look. "I fired on the bear, but only hurt him enough to make him ugly. I fell right over him while I was after a deer I had wounded some time before."

"Oh, then you were the hunter we heard shoot," said Todd. "The deer got away, eh?"

"Yes, I lost track of the deer when I hit the bear," answered the cowboy from the Merwell ranch. "I'm mighty glad you came up!" he added to Dave.

"It's all right, I am glad I did too," answered the youth. "I was wishing I'd get a chance at a bear." He saw that Snogger was deeply affected, and was swallowing a lump that came up in his throat.

"And to think it was you, boy!" went on the cowboy, feelingly. "You—and after what I did to you!"

"Let us forget that, Snogger."

"I ain't going to forgit it. I was a low-down hound, that's what I was," said the man, with energy. "I listened to what that Link Merwell had to say against you, and I planned to do you all the harm I could,—jest to please that fellow."

"Hank, you made a mistake to go over to Merwell," put in Sid Todd. "I don't like to hit at a fellow when he's hurted, but I've got to speak my mind."

"Well, you are only telling the truth," answered Snogger, shortly. "I know it as well as you do. I'm going to quit Merwell the first chance I git."

Dave and Todd made Snogger as comfortable as possible, and the cowboy said he would be all right after he got his wind back. Then Todd went off to locate Roger and Phil and

Edward Stratemeyer

apprise them of what had occurred.

"Mr. Snogger, I'd like to ask you a question," said Dave, when the two were alone and the man was resting comfortably against a tree. "You look very much like a boy I and my friends met in Chicago. Do you know the lad? His name is Charley Gamp."

"Charley Gamp!" exclaimed the man, and stared wildly at Dave. "Say, what do you know about him?"

"Then you know him?" And now Dave was deeply interested.

"Do I know him! He is my son!"

"Your son? Then where did the name Gamp come from?"

"Gamp was his mother's name afore she married me. Tell me, is he safe?"

"Yes." And then Dave related how he and the others had fallen in with Charley at the post-office.

"And Link Merwell was abusin' him—callin' him a thief!" cried Hank Snogger, and his eyes commenced to blaze. "How did he dare! Why, Link Merwell is a thief himself!"

"A thief!" echoed Dave.

"Yes. But let that pass now—I'll tell you later. Tell me of my boy, my Charley," pleaded Hank Snogger.

Dave told all that he knew, and the man listened eagerly. Then Snogger told something of his life's history, how he and his wife had quarreled and how some neighbors had gotten them to separate. He had drifted to the West, and remained there for three years. Then he had gone back to look for his wife, but had found out that she was dead. He could get no trace of his little boy, and finally had gone West again. At first he had carried himself straight, but presently he had gotten in with the wrong set and had drank and gambled, and left Mr. Endicott to go to work for Mr. Merwell.

"But I am going to turn over a new leaf," he said. "Only let me find my boy! I'll show him what a good father I can be to him!" And his face took on a look of hope.

"And now I am going to tell you about Link Merwell," went on Hank Snogger, a little later. "I feel you ought to know, for you are the one who has suffered most because of his doings. You remember how your horses were stolen."

"Yes."

"Well, Link took 'em. He says he didn't mean to steal 'em, but that is what it amounted to. He took 'em, and while the storm was on some cattle-thieves, headed by Andy Andrews, came along. Link says Andrews and his gang took the horses away, but I think Link made a deal with the hoss-thieves, for the next day I see Link with a roll of bank-bills, and I know Mr. Merwell didn't give him the money. He had about two hundred dollars, and I think he got the wad from Andrews—on his promise not to open his mouth."

"How did you learn this?"

"I was out, rounding up some stray steers, and I saw him just before the storm with the hosses. I wasn't near enough to talk to him, but that night I spoke to him, and he couldn't deny that he took 'em in the first place. He was terribly afraid I'd give him away, and he said if I did he'd say I took 'em. Well, you can believe me or not, but he took 'em."

"I believe you," answered Dave. "And we'll have this matter sifted just as soon as we return to Star Ranch."

It was some time ere Todd, Roger, and Phil showed themselves. In the meantime Dave made Snogger promise not to say anything about the stolen horses to the others.

"Perhaps the matter can be fixed up between Mr. Endicott and Mr. Merwell," he said. "It would be terrible to have Link publicly branded as a horse-thief."

Hank Snogger had been out alone and he readily consented to join the others at their camp. The two elk and the bear were brought in, and it was decided to start back for the ranches the next morning.

"I must see Mr. Endicott on important business," said Dave to Sid Todd, and then, in private, he told his chums what he had heard concerning Link Merwell. Todd was told about Charley Gamp, and said he hoped that the finding of the son would make a new man of Snogger.

The return to the ranches was begun at sunrise. They carried with them the skin of the bear and also the pelts and heads of the elk. They camped that night in the foothills, and reached Star Ranch about noon the next day.

"I want you to come with me," said Dave to Hank Snogger, after the boys had received a warm greeting from the girls and Mrs. Endicott. And he led the way to Mr. Endicott's office, a small affair located in the ranch home. Here the cowboy told his story once more, just as he had related it to Dave.

"I have suspected something of this sort all along," said Mr. Endicott. "One of our own men saw young Merwell with some horses on that day, but he was not sure if they were our animals. Andrews took the horses up into Canada and sold them at several places, so I don't think I'll be able to get them back. But, if I can prove Link guilty, I shall most certainly hold his father responsible."

Hank Snogger was anxious to go East, to find his son, but was persuaded to remain where he was until the young folks should bring their visit to an end. In the meantime, however, a telegram was sent to Charley and he sent one in return, stating he would be glad to meet his parent.

"Dave, you can go with me to the Merwell house," said Mr. Endicott the next day. "And you can go, too, Snogger."

The three set out, and when within sight of the other ranch home they caught sight of Link Merwell, riding slowly along on his pony. He scowled as he recognized them.

"What do you want here?" he asked, looking at Dave.

"We came for our horses," answered Dave, boldly.

At these words Link grew pale and shot a swift glance at Hank Snogger. Then, in a sudden rage, he shook his fist at the cowboy.

"What have you been saying about me?" he cried angrily.

"Telling the truth," answered Snogger.

"It's false! I didn't touch the horses!" gasped Link, but he grew whiter than ever.

"You took them, and you might as well confess," said Mr. Endicott, sternly. "If you won't confess, and get your father to square up, I'll call on the sheriff of this county to arrest you."

"I—I—didn't mean—that is—I—" commenced Link, and then he broke down completely. He acknowledged that he had taken the horses, but said he did it in fun. Then the cattle-thieves had come along and taken the steeds from him.

"And you got paid for letting them go," said Mr. Endicott. "You got several hundred dollars from Andrews."

"Who say—says so?" faltered Link.

"Never mind, we'll prove it," answered the railroad president, coldly.

"I only got seventy-five dollars!" shouted Link. "I—I didn't sell the horses. Andrews gave me that money because—because—" And then he stopped short, not knowing how to go on.

"He gave you the money so you would keep silent," said Dave.

"We have heard enough—come to the house," said Mr. Endicott, and against his will, Link was made to accompany the others back to his home.

Mr. Merwell was met at the door, and a bitter quarrel took place in his office, lasting the best part of an hour. At first the ranch owner would not believe his son was guilty, but when he saw Link break down he had to give in. He said he would pay for the horses that had been stolen, and also pay to have the whole matter hushed up.

"You cannot pay me for hushing the matter up," said Mr. Endicott. "I have no desire to ruin your son's future. If you will pay for the horses, that is all I ask—that and one thing more. I have no desire to live next door to a man who has a son who is a horse-thief. I understand that you have received a good offer for your ranch. My advice is that you sell out."

"I will!" snapped Mr. Merwell. "I'll get out just as soon as the title can be passed! I never liked to live here, anyway!" And then in a rage he made out a check for the value of the horses, handed it to Mr. Endicott, and showed his visitors to the door.

"Phew, but he was mad!" was Dave's comment, as the three rode over to Star Ranch.

"If he sells out, that is all I ask," said Mr. Endicott. It may be added here that, two weeks later, Mr. Merwell sold his place and moved to parts unknown, taking his son with him. The purchaser of the ranch proved to be an agreeable man, and he and Mr. Endicott got along very well together.

"Well, I hope that is the last of Link Merwell," said Roger, when he heard about the affair. But it was not the last of the fellow, as Dave, later on, found out. Link crossed his path again, and what happened will be told in the next volume of this series, to be called, "Dave Porter and His Rivals; or, The Chums and Foes of Oak Hall." In that volume we shall meet all our old friends and learn the particulars of a peculiar mystery and a stirring struggle on the gridiron.

At last came the time to leave Star Ranch. Mr. Dunston Porter arrived, and listened to the many tales the young folks had to tell.

"Well, you certainly have crowded things," he declared. "I wish I had been on that hunt."

Belle was going East with Laura and Jessie, and Snogger accompanied the boys and Mr. Porter. All received a warm send-off at the railroad station.

"Come again!" shouted Sid Todd, and to show his spirits fired his revolver into the air, and the other cowboys did the same.

At Chicago the party were met by Charley Gamp. Hank Snogger hugged his boy to his breast and wept for joy, and Charley cried too, and so did the girls. Then it was learned that Snogger was really a carpenter by trade. He said he would settle down in the city, and did so, and to-day he is a steady workman, and he and Charley have a good home. The father is giving the son a good education, hoping to make a first-class business man of him.

"Well, all told, we had the outing of our lives," declared Roger, on the way to Crumville.

"It couldn't have been better!" cried Dave. "I tell you what, Star Ranch is all right!"

And the others agreed with him. And here, for the time being, let us say farewell.

THE END

Choose from Thousands of 1stWorldLibrary Classics By

A. M. Barnard	Booth Tarkington	Edward Everett Hale
Ada Leverson	Boyd Cable	Edward J. O'Biren
Adolphus William Ward	Bram Stoker	Edward S. Ellis
Aesop	C. Collodi	Edwin L. Arnold
Agatha Christie	C. E. Orr	Eleanor Atkins
Alexander Aaronsohn	C. M. Ingleby	Eleanor Hallowell Abbott
Alexander Kielland	Carolyn Wells	Eliot Gregory
Alexandre Dumas	Catherine Parr Traill	Elizabeth Gaskell
Alfred Gatty	Charles A. Eastman	Elizabeth McCracken
Alfred Ollivant	Charles Amory Beach	Elizabeth Von Arnim
Alice Duer Miller	Charles Dickens	Ellem Key
Alice Turner Curtis	Charles Dudley Warner	Emerson Hough
Alice Dunbar	Charles Farrar Browne	Emilie F. Carlen
Allen Chapman	Charles Ives	Emily Bronte
Alleyne Ireland	Charles Kingsley	Emily Dickinson
Ambrose Bierce	Charles Klein	Enid Bagnold
Amelia E. Barr	Charles Hanson Towne	Enilor Macartney Lane
Amory H. Bradford	Charles Lathrop Pack	Erasmus W. Jones
Andrew Lang	Charles Romyn Dake	Ernie Howard Pie
Andrew McFarland Davis	Charles Whibley	Ethel May Dell
Andy Adams	Charles Willing Beale	Ethel Turner
Angela Brazil	Charlotte M. Braeme	Ethel Watts Mumford
Anna Alice Chapin	Charlotte M. Yonge	Eugene Sue
Anna Sewell	Charlotte Perkins Stetson	Eugenie Foa
Annie Besant	Clair W. Hayes	Eugene Wood
Annie Hamilton Donnell	Clarence Day Jr.	Eustace Hale Ball
Annie Payson Call	Clarence E. Mulford	Evelyn Everett-green
Annie Roe Carr	Clemence Housman	Everard Cotes
Annonaymous	Confucius	F. H. Cheley
Anton Chekhov	Coningsby Dawson	F. J. Cross
Archibald Lee Fletcher	Cornelis DeWitt Wilcox	F. Marion Crawford
Arnold Bennett	Cyril Burleigh	Fannie E. Newberry
Arthur C. Benson	D. H. Lawrence	Federick Austin Ogg
Arthur Conan Doyle	Daniel Defoe	Ferdinand Ossendowski
Arthur M. Winfield	David Garnett	Fergus Hume
Arthur Ransome	Dinah Craik	Florence A. Kilpatrick
Arthur Schnitzler	Don Carlos Janes	Fremont B. Deering
Arthur Train	Donald Keyhoe	Francis Bacon
Atticus	Dorothy Kilner	Francis Darwin
B.H. Baden-Powell	Dougan Clark	Frances Hodgson Burnett
B. M. Bower	Douglas Fairbanks	Frances Parkinson Keyes
B. C. Chatterjee	E. Nesbit	Frank Gee Patchin
Baroness Emmuska Orczy	E. P. Roe	Frank Harris
Baroness Orczy	E. Phillips Oppenheim	Frank Jewett Mather
Basil King	E. S. Brooks	Frank L. Packard
Bayard Taylor	Earl Barnes	Frank V. Webster
Ben Macomber	Edgar Rice Burroughs	Frederic Stewart Isham
Bertha Muzzy Bower	Edith Van Dyne	Frederick Trevor Hill
Bjornstjerne Bjornson	Edith Wharton	Frederick Winslow Taylor

Friedrich Kerst
Friedrich Nietzsche
Fyodor Dostoyevsky
G.A. Henty
G.K. Chesterton
Gabrielle E. Jackson
Garrett P. Serviss
Gaston Leroux
George A. Warren
George Ade
Geroge Bernard Shaw
George Cary Eggleston
George Durston
George Ebers
George Eliot
George Gissing
George MacDonald
George Meredith
George Orwell
George Sylvester Viereck
George Tucker
George W. Cable
George Wharton James
Gertrude Atherton
Gordon Casserly
Grace E. King
Grace Gallatin
Grace Greenwood
Grant Allen
Guillermo A. Sherwell
Gulielma Zollinger
Gustav Flaubert
H. A. Cody
H. B. Irving
H.C. Bailey
H. G. Wells
H. H. Munro
H. Irving Hancock
H. R. Naylor
H. Rider Haggard
H. W. C. Davis
Haldeman Julius
Hall Caine
Hamilton Wright Mabie
Hans Christian Andersen
Harold Avery
Harold McGrath
Harriet Beecher Stowe
Harry Castlemon
Harry Coghill
Harry Houidini

Hayden Carruth
Helent Hunt Jackson
Helen Nicolay
Hendrik Conscience
Hendy David Thoreau
Henri Barbusse
Henrik Ibsen
Henry Adams
Henry Ford
Henry Frost
Henry James
Henry Jones Ford
Henry Seton Merriman
Henry W Longfellow
Herbert A. Giles
Herbert Carter
Herbert N. Casson
Herman Hesse
Hildegard G. Frey
Homer
Honore De Balzac
Horace B. Day
Horace Walpole
Horatio Alger Jr.
Howard Pyle
Howard R. Garis
Hugh Lofting
Hugh Walpole
Humphry Ward
Ian Maclaren
Inez Haynes Gillmore
Irving Bacheller
Isabel Cecilia Williams
Isabel Hornibrook
Israel Abrahams
Ivan Turgenev
J.G.Austin
J. Henri Fabre
J. M. Barrie
J. M. Walsh
J. Macdonald Oxley
J. R. Miller
J. S. Fletcher
J. S. Knowles
J. Storer Clouston
J. W. Duffield
Jack London
Jacob Abbott
James Allen
James Andrews
James Baldwin

James Branch Cabell
James DeMille
James Joyce
James Lane Allen
James Lane Allen
James Oliver Curwood
James Oppenheim
James Otis
James R. Driscoll
Jane Abbott
Jane Austen
Jane L. Stewart
Janet Aldridge
Jens Peter Jacobsen
Jerome K. Jerome
Jessie Graham Flower
John Buchan
John Burroughs
John Cournos
John F. Kennedy
John Gay
John Glasworthy
John Habberton
John Joy Bell
John Kendrick Bangs
John Milton
John Philip Sousa
John Taintor Foote
Jonas Lauritz Idemil Lie
Jonathan Swift
Joseph A. Altsheler
Joseph Carey
Joseph Conrad
Joseph E. Badger Jr
Joseph Hergesheimer
Joseph Jacobs
Jules Vernes
Julian Hawthrone
Julie A Lippmann
Justin Huntly McCarthy
Kakuzo Okakura
Karle Wilson Baker
Kate Chopin
Kenneth Grahame
Kenneth McGaffey
Kate Langley Bosher
Kate Langley Bosher
Katherine Cecil Thurston
Katherine Stokes
L. A. Abbot
L. T. Meade

L. Frank Baum
Latta Griswold
Laura Dent Crane
Laura Lee Hope
Laurence Housman
Lawrence Beasley
Leo Tolstoy
Leonid Andreyev
Lewis Carroll
Lewis Sperry Chafer
Lilian Bell
Lloyd Osbourne
Louis Hughes
Louis Joseph Vance
Louis Tracy
Louisa May Alcott
Lucy Fitch Perkins
Lucy Maud Montgomery
Luther Benson
Lydia Miller Middleton
Lyndon Orr
M. Corvus
M. H. Adams
Margaret E. Sangster
Margret Howth
Margaret Vandercook
Margaret W. Hungerford
Margret Penrose
Maria Edgeworth
Maria Thompson Daviess
Mariano Azuela
Marion Polk Angellotti
Mark Overton
Mark Twain
Mary Austin
Mary Catherine Crowley
Mary Cole
Mary Hastings Bradley
Mary Roberts Rinehart
Mary Rowlandson
M. Wollstonecraft Shelley
Maud Lindsay
Max Beerbohm
Myra Kelly
Nathaniel Hawthrone
Nicolo Machiavelli
O. F. Walton
Oscar Wilde

Owen Johnson
P.G. Wodehouse
Paul and Mabel Thorne
Paul G. Tomlinson
Paul Severing
Percy Brebner
Percy Keese Fitzhugh
Peter B. Kyne
Plato
Quincy Allen
R. Derby Holmes
R. L. Stevenson
R. S. Ball
Rabindranath Tagore
Rahul Alvares
Ralph Bonehill
Ralph Henry Barbour
Ralph Victor
Ralph Waldo Emmerson
Rene Descartes
Ray Cummings
Rex Beach
Rex E. Beach
Richard Harding Davis
Richard Jefferies
Richard Le Gallienne
Robert Barr
Robert Frost
Robert Gordon Anderson
Robert L. Drake
Robert Lansing
Robert Lynd
Robert Michael Ballantyne
Robert W. Chambers
Rosa Nouchette Carey
Rudyard Kipling
Saint Augustine
Samuel B. Allison
Samuel Hopkins Adams
Sarah Bernhardt
Sarah C. Hallowell
Selma Lagerlof
Sherwood Anderson
Sigmund Freud
Standish O'Grady
Stanley Weyman
Stella Benson
Stella M. Francis

Stephen Crane
Stewart Edward White
Stijn Streuvels
Swami Abhedananda
Swami Parmananda
T. S. Ackland
T. S. Arthur
The Princess Der Ling
Thomas A. Janvier
Thomas A Kempis
Thomas Anderton
Thomas Bailey Aldrich
Thomas Bulfinch
Thomas De Quincey
Thomas Dixon
Thomas H. Huxley
Thomas Hardy
Thomas More
Thornton W. Burgess
U. S. Grant
Upton Sinclair
Valentine Williams
Various Authors
Vaughan Kester
Victor Appleton
Victor G. Durham
Victoria Cross
Virginia Woolf
Wadsworth Camp
Walter Camp
Walter Scott
Washington Irving
Wilbur Lawton
Wilkie Collins
Willa Cather
Willard F. Baker
William Dean Howells
William le Queux
W. Makepeace Thackeray
William W. Walter
William Shakespeare
Winston Churchill
Yei Theodora Ozaki
Yogi Ramacharaka
Young E. Allison
Zane Grey